D1255112

10.95

McCutchan
Orders for Cameron

DATE DUE			
NO 4 '83	JE 21 '85		
DE 7 '83	JE 18 '85		
MR 3 '84	SE 6 '85		
MR 23 '84	DE 4 '85		
MY 25 '84	FE 3 '89		
AG 1 '84			
AG 22 '84			
SE 28 '84			
NO 21 '84			
JA 30 '85			
AP 9 '85			

EB

Orders for Cameron

Featuring Lieutenant St Vincent Halfhyde, RN:
Beware, Beware the Bight of Benin
Halfhyde's Island
The Guns of Arrest
Halfhyde to the Narrows
Halfhyde for the Queen
Halfhyde Ordered South
Halfhyde and the Flag Captain
Halfhyde on Zanatu

Featuring Donald Cameron:
Cameron in the Gap

Orders for Cameron

Philip McCutchan

St. Martin's Press
New York

231900

ORDERS FOR CAMERON. Copyright © 1983 by Philip McCutchan.
All rights reserved. Printed in the United States of America.
No part of this book may be used or reproduced in any
manner whatsoever without written permission except in the
case of brief quotations embodied in critical articles or reviews.
For information, address St. Martin's Press, 175 Fifth Avenue,
New York, N.Y. 10010.

Library of Congress Cataloging in Publication Data

McCutchan, Philip, 1920-
   Orders for Cameron.

   1. World War, 1939-1945 — Fiction. I. Title.
PR6063.A16707   1983   823'.914   83-9601
ISBN 0-312-58722-8

First published in Great Britain by Arthur Barker Limited.

First U.S. Edition

10 9 8 7 6 5 4 3 2 1

g-83 Baker 6.79

1

IT was a brightly moonlit night. Off the West African coast the sea was flat, moving only to a swell coming in across the South Atlantic to end in surf on the white sandy beaches beyond the eastern horizon, cut by the tumbling wakes of the warships on passage north from Freetown in Sierra Leone to the Gibraltar Strait. From the bridge of *HM Corvette Oleander*, Donald Cameron, First Lieutenant and currently officer of the middle watch, scanned the dark horizons all around as the moon unkindly lit the escort's charges: *Oleander* was stationed on the port bow of *HMS Wiltshire*, a three-funnelled County-class cruiser. Behind *Wiltshire* was a 17,000-ton depot ship of new construction, *HMS Mars*. Both these ships had come up from the Cape, and when their escort had broken off into Freetown, *Oleander* and her sister ship, *Forsythia*, had taken over together with the destroyer *Halberdier*, the latter now guarding the rear of the heavy ships.

Cameron turned as he heard footsteps on the starboard ladder: a bulky duffel-coated figure clambered onto the bridge. 'Morning, Cameron. And damn the bloody moon for a start.'

'Good morning, sir. And I agree about the moon. It's bad luck.'

The Captain, Lieutenant-Commander John Forrest, RNR, gave a moody grunt. 'You'll agree more soon, Cameron. There's been a cypher from the Admiralty. They've counted twenty-one U-boats on the plot – slap bang between us and the Straits. Young Lightwell looked as

1

though he'd given birth to kittens when he showed me the plain-language transcript. I'm going to first degree of readiness – just in case. Don't use the alarm rattlers, send the boatswain's mate to pipe round below. And warn the engine-room.'

'Aye, aye, sir.' Bending to the voice-pipe, Cameron passed the orders down to the quartermaster in the wheel-house. Then, using the sound-powered telephone, he called the Engine-Room Artificer on watch. Finding that the Chief ERA himself was unexpectedly on the starting platform, he said, 'Trouble ahead, Chief. Did you kind of smell it out, or what?'

'I reckon I did, sir. Just what is it, eh?'

Cameron told him. Back came a stream of semi-respectful blasphemy. What Chief ERA Makin would like to do to all U-boat commanders was nobody's business. Cameron cut the call and resumed his careful watch. To port and star-board the lookouts scanned their arcs, watching through their binoculars for the tell-tale feather of water that would indicate a periscope raised to just above the surface. Twenty-one U-boats gave a potential promise of one hell of a lot of torpedoes and it had now become obvious that something had leaked. This was not too surprising, of course, consider-ing the vast scale of the forthcoming operation, the almost world-wide movements of ships and troops and armour con-verging on the Straits of Gibraltar. The U-boats would not be in position simply to mount an attack on the *Wiltshire* and the *Mars*; there were numbers of vessels still coming up from Simonstown in convoy. But the heavy ships were a worth-while target, one not to be let through unscathed; the *Mars* in particular was much needed in the port of Algiers to act as parent ship for the destroyers and smaller craft that would be piling into the Mediterranean.

The date was 2 November 1942; and in six days' time the combined British and American seaborne invasion of North Africa was due to start.

It had been West Africa's rainy season when Cameron had joined *Oleander* a couple of months earlier, taking passage from the Clyde in a battleship bound for the Cape and the Indian Ocean. On arrival he had found the corvette absent at sea, and had been accommodated in the old *Edinburgh Castle*, a former Union Castle liner now in naval service and in use as a depot ship. She was so elderly as to be almost falling to pieces, was full of rats and cockroaches and was foetid below, especially for those, like Cameron, who were unlucky enough to be allotted an inboard cabin. On the upper deck it was a case of virtually continuous rain, a heavy, vicious downpour that soaked a white uniform in two seconds flat. The air, what there was of it, was close, suffocatingly so. Cameron was accompanied by another officer for the *Oleander*: the corvette had suffered casualties in surface action with a U-boat prowling the northern part of the South Atlantic, her First Lieutenant and a sub-lieutenant having been killed. Cameron's companion was Sub-Lieutenant Rufus Lightwell, a bookish young man who had been reading for an arts degree at Cambridge until war had called and he had volunteered for the Navy – somewhat surprisingly, since he had been seasick aboard the battleship all the way from the Clyde. Cameron had scarcely seen him until they had been put aboard the *Edinburgh Castle* in the calm flatness of the Rokel River.

Lightwell was a brand-new officer, just out of the *King Alfred* training establishment at Hove in Sussex. His first real utterance to Cameron, made as the battleship's motor-cutter took them across to the depot ship in pouring rain, was scarcely nautical. He said reflectively, '*Oleander*.'

'Quite. So what?'

Lightwell turned a serious face on him. 'I've been looking it up in the *Shorter Oxford*.'

'It's a flower. She's a Flower-class corvette.'

'Ah! You and I might differ as to what constitutes a flower, I think – '

'You and I and the Admiralty.'

3

'Yes. An oleander isn't a flower, it's a *shrub*. I quote the dictionary: an evergreen poisonous Levantine shrub with leathery lanceolate leaves and fine red and white flowers.' Lightwell looked disconsolate. 'Poisonous!'

Cameron grinned. 'Well, at least it's evergreen. I dare say we shall survive.'

'I hope so. It's all a bit of a nuisance really. I hope Christ's will take me back when it's all over.' Lightwell gave a sigh. 'It'd be sickening if everything's different after the war.'

'What were you going to do?' Cameron asked.

'History.'

'Yes. I didn't quite mean that. What were you going to be?'

'Be?' Lightwell looked blank, and his eyebrows rose.

'Your career.'

'Good heavens, I've really no idea. One has to browse, to ponder. A career needs a good deal of thought.'

If they were all like Lightwell, undergraduates must be a weird bunch, was Cameron's thought. Lightwell would get scant chance to ponder aboard a corvette, anyway; scant time to do anything but keep his watch, perform the many other duties of a junior officer, and catch up on sleep when possible. In Lightwell's somewhat heavy-going company Cameron passed four days aboard the *Edinburgh Castle*, four days eased by lunch-time and evening gin in the wardroom – Lightwell drinking only squash – and then during the fifth forenoon he watched the *Oleander* enter harbour looking seaworn with rust-marks beneath her hawse-pipes. As First Lieutenant it would be one of his jobs, as soon as time permitted, to see to that: some red lead and a coat of paint applied by men working over the side from bosun's chairs would soon smarten her up. Maybe not even bosun's chairs: the corvette hadn't much freeboard and the hands could work from a boat . . . the *Oleander* was no great battleship or cruiser.

On reporting aboard Cameron was met on the tiny quart-erdeck by an older-than-average RNVR lieutenant who introduced himself as Perry-Grant, an officer who seemed to be a prey to his nerves: his face had a curious twitch and his eyes were ever on the move, right and left and up and down. He seemed suspicious and unwelcoming. Father, he said, would see Cameron right away; and he took the new First Lieutenant personally to the Captain's cabin.

A big man got to his feet, smiling pleasantly. Cameron saw on the shoulders of the white tropical shirt the intertwined gold stripes of the RNR with a thin straight stripe between. Lieutenant-Commander Forrest looked a no-nonsense man; and his manner of speaking was direct and abrupt.

'Cameron,' he said, an eye going briefly to the ribbon of the DSC on his First Lieutenant's number ten jacket: Cameron had decided on the formality of full whites for the occasion of joining. 'Glad to have you aboard. All right, Grant, thank you,' he added in an aside, and Perry-Grant backed out of the cabin. Forrest grinned at Cameron and gestured him to a chair. 'Polite of you to dress,' he said. 'You'll be glad to get out of that rig, though, and you can do so as soon as you like. We wear thirteens *all* the time.'

'Right, sir.'

The Captain glanced at the clock: it was just after noon. 'Gin?'

'Thank you, sir.'

Forrest shouted for his steward, and gin was brought, two small ones with lime-juice. The Captain talked about his ship, in which he had an obvious pride. Small but tough, he said, go anywhere, do anything. That was what corvettes were all about. But it could get boring and at the end of an escort job there was only Freetown to come back to, Freetown being the tropical equivalent of Scapa in the north of Scotland. There were only two places to go for relaxation, one being the Colonial officers' club up at the hill station where you could play billiards, the other an apology for an English pub called the Lion and Palm Tree officially but known by a cruder name to the Navy. And if you didn't mind picking up a dose of foot rot that would last you the rest of your life, you could swim at Lumley beach. But their current purpose in life was the same as almost all the rest of the Navy: convoy escort, in their case to and from Gibraltar and now and again down to the Cape, at neither destination spending longer in port than was absolutely necessary to embark fuel and stores and replace ammunition for the guns and depth charges. Escorts were always in short supply. There was, however, the occasional boiler-clean when the ship had a blessed fourteen-day spell in civilization, though sometimes some demon of efficiency entered the dockyard mateys and they turned her out quicker.

After another glance at the clock Forrest stood up. He said, 'Well, that's enough gas. If you're feeling generous, you can invite me along to the wardroom tonight and stand *me* a gin. At that time, I'll expect you to have familiarized yourself with the ship, all right?'

'Yes, sir.'

Forrest gave him a square look and said, 'You've a good record. I'm lucky to have you as my Number One. That being said, I'll spare your blushes. There's just one thing more and it's between you and me. I hope you'll not think I'm telling tales out of school – I'm not, but it has to be said since you've a right to know the score. It's this. Perry-Grant, to give him the full works which I don't normally, is suffering badly from not being made Number One himself. There's temperament around ... I don't suggest there's necessarily a connection, but he was a barrister in civil life. You'll have to watch your step. He's some years older than you and has been acting Number One – we didn't expect someone senior to him by a couple of months to be appointed. His nose is out of joint and in any case I don't find him up to the job. That's all I have to say, and it won't be mentioned again. Off you go – and send in that new sub, will you?'

Cameron found Lightwell and passed the order. He hoped the Sub wouldn't be telling the Captain he commanded a poisonous ship.

Boredom did indeed set in; one convoy escort was much like another although there were the occasional battles with U-boats. *Oleander* and *Forsythia* came through with more kills to their credit and with no loss to their own ships' companies. Despite the appalling rain that afflicted them most of the time whilst within the climatic orbit of Freetown, Cameron found it a good deal more relaxed and comfortable than either the North Atlantic or the Russian convoys. Then, as the weeks went past into late October, something began to disturb the semi-somnolent air of the Freetown base. More and more convoys entered and each one seemed to contain more ships and heavier escort forces than its predecessor. Rumours abounded; the BBC Overseas News spoke of wondrous happenings in North Africa, of Monty pushing westwards from El Alamein with what seemed to be his unstoppable Eighth Army of Desert Rats. With luck, the fortunes of the war might be on the change. Battleships came and went: *Rodney* and *Nelson*, backing up the convoy escorts with the tremendous power of their 16-inch turrets, and *Revenge* with her 15-inch guns. Suddenly, Freetown was very much more obviously on the map. Even the Kroos, the local native fishermen some of whom were locally and temporarily enlisted into the Navy to serve aboard the depot ship, seemed to sense that things were stirring; and the dug-out canoes, the bumboats that came out for the fleecing of British sailors until they were driven off by the wash-deck hoses, brought excited traders who increased the pressure of their salesmanship as though they knew that the ships would soon be withdrawn from the river. Even the *Edinburgh Castle* seethed with rumours that she might be about to brave the open seas again in proof that she hadn't settled forever on her own jettisoned tin cans and bottles.

Then one forenoon the Captain was bidden by signal to attend upon the Flag Officer, West Africa. When he came back aboard he was clutching a large brown envelope, bare of any markings. Cameron met him at the accommodation-ladder and was told to report to his cabin in ten minutes' time. When he did so, the Captain had stripped off the outer envelope to reveal an inner one, heavily marked ON HIS MAJESTY'S SERVICE and bearing the classification MOST SECRET: FOR THE EYES OF OFFICERS ONLY.

He patted the envelope and said, 'There you are, Cameron. In time, all becomes revealed.'

'What is it, sir?'

'TSGO,' Forrest said unhelpfully, then added, 'Torch Secret General Orders. It's what we've all been waiting for: the invasion of North Africa, in support of Montgomery.'

There were pages and pages of it: an extraordinarily detailed document covering hundreds of ships, tens of thousands of men both British and American, great volumes of stores and oil fuel, armour, gun batteries, stocks of ammunition; all to converge shortly upon Gibraltar and then move through the Straits for two main areas of attack: Oran and Algiers, with a third landing planned for outside the Straits at Casablanca in Morocco, this to be achieved by the American land and sea forces. The British Naval escort and troop-support commands would be split into two, the Eastern Task force under Vice-Admiral Sir Harold Burrough and the Central Task Force under Commodore Troubridge, while an American, Rear Admiral Hewitt, took charge of the Western Task Force at Casablanca; and while General Eisenhower had the supreme authority as Allied C-in-C the whole of the seaborne assault would be under the overall command of Admiral Sir Andrew Cunningham, designated Naval Commander Expeditionary Force.

'NCXF for short,' Forrest said, and shook his head in awe. 'Every damn contingency is covered and everything slots in no matter what. Good weather, bad weather, late arrivals here and there, sinkings of vital ships en route necessitating a reshuffle ... even the possibility, I shouldn't wonder, of the Captain of *Rodney* developing piles at the last moment. It's a work of bloody art, no less. Thank God I didn't have to work it all out. I'm just a simple sailor. The planners must have minds like crossword puzzles. Not far short of the entire blasted Navy's involved. Even us.' He paused, then went on, 'We're going to have corrections as things develop and ships detailed get sunk and the alternatives are brought into play. I'll see to what I can myself, but I'll need reliable assistance. You're going to be too busy getting the ship ready for all this. How's young Lightwell coming along?'

'Fair enough, sir. I think you'll agree, he's becoming competent on the bridge.'

'Yes, he is. But this isn't bridge watchkeeping, Number One. It's patient, dogged paperwork and God help anyone who makes a balls and gets, say, a call-sign or radio frequency wrong. Or an identification signal. Get it?'

Cameron nodded. 'Yes, sir. Lightwell's been studying at Cambridge. Paperwork's his forte, I imagine.'

Forrest grunted. 'Cambridge . . . I knew that. But is it all study and bookwork at Cambridge, I wonder? Or is it mostly booze and women?'

'Not in Lightwell's case, sir.'

'No, I take your point! All right, send him along and I'll stress that I'll have his liver out if he gets so much as a comma out of place. Young Kollenborne can assist him – as one of our next-war admirals, the planning practice should do him good!' Kollenborne was a midshipman RN. 'And remember, Number One – not a mention of this to anyone else at all. I'm not a man who usually goes by the book, but this time I've got to – at this stage I can't even confide in the Chief, seeing he's not an officer. However, that's my worry.'

'Yes, sir. Any orders in the meantime, sir?'

'Just this: see to all stores and so on – ammo, provisions, deck gear, anything that strikes you. I'm standing by for our personal orders and they could come at any time even though TSGO says we and *Forsythia* leave for Gib on the twenty-ninth – two days' time. I'm thinking of all those alternatives. Any trouble with the shore, let me know and I'll make a song and dance. The base paymaster's already buzzing around like a blue-arsed fly that's taken a dose of caster oil.'

2

NONE of the alternatives came about insofar as *Oleander* was concerned: she left Freetown on 29 October as laid down in Torch Secret General Orders to pick up her charges outside the river. Cameron, who had had a busy forty-eight hours seeing the ship made ready for whatever might come to her in the days and weeks ahead, was standing in the eyes of the ship as Government Wharf and King Tom Pier faded away astern on the port quarter. The day was blindingly hot; the rains were petering out now and the sun was ferocious, causing steam from the land to rise around the thickly-growing palm trees. The dug-out canoes with their gesticulating occupants were left behind in the wakes of *Oleander* and *Forsythia*. Cameron had a feeling he would not be seeing Freetown again; if all went well with Torch the balance of the war would be shifted nearer home, and the Mediterranean Fleet under Cunningham would need all available resources to retain its re-established grip on the Middle Sea.

As for Freetown itself, he had no regrets on leaving.

Nor, it seemed, had the lower deck. A voice came to Cameron as the order was passed for the hands to fall out from stations and he moved aft to climb to the bridge. It was the voice of the buffer, Petty Officer Osbaldston. 'Bloody 'ole. Know what? It's not only t'world's backside, it's two miles bloody oop it!'

Cameron grinned to himself and passed on. It was near enough two miles from Lumley beach to Cape Sierra Leone and the open sea. When he reached the bridge, however, he

11

found the Captain, who had also overheard the loud comment, less appreciative of the witticism than apprehensive of a leak in security. Forrest took him aside and said in a low voice, 'I didn't care for the sound of that, Number One.'

'Sailors will be sailors, sir.'

'Go and teach your grandmother. What I meant was that I detected an undercurrent. Osbaldston sounded as though he was saying goodbye for good – and it's not supposed to be known we're not coming back.'

'I doubt if it matters much now, sir.'

Forrest said impatiently, 'Maybe not, so far as we are concerned – in fact I'll be telling the ship's company the score, or some of it, after we take over the escort. What bothers me is that things may have spread ashore. Or maybe I'm just getting over-conscious of security in my old age.'

Cameron didn't comment. He understood the Captain's anxieties well enough. Already there had been some mishaps that could undermine the operation, which in any case had been subject to a couple of delays. Initially Torch had been planned to start on 30 October, and during September this date had been put forward to 4 November and subsequently again postponed to the eighth, largely on account of United States requirements. And some private information had been passed to Forrest by the Flag Officer ashore; Forrest had passed this on to Cameron: in late September a Catalina aircraft, coming to grief in the water off the south coast of Spain, had discharged the body of a British officer who had happened to be carrying documents concerned with Torch and giving the then current invasion date as 4 November. It was believed that this body had been washed on to the Spanish coast in the vicinity of Cadiz. Spain, or at any rate its southern coast, was well known to be crawling with Hitler's spies. But, even though the fact of the operation could well have been compromised, the decision had been taken to adhere to the final date of 8 November. When the armadas began to pass through the Straits of Gibraltar, the enemy was going to know in any case; there would be many binoculars trained on the troop convoys.

Once *Oleander* had taken up her station on the port bow of the *Wiltshire* and the sloops from the Cape had turned away to enter the river, the Captain had all off-watch hands mustered on the fo'c'sle and addressed them from the bridge.

He said, 'We're bound for the Straits. That's all I'm permitted to tell you – that we shall not be returning to Freetown.' He waited while the information was given the cheer it deserved, then held up a hand for quiet. 'We shall enter Gibraltar to take on oil fuel and make up stores but shore leave will not be granted. Our stay in Gibraltar will be minimal. After we leave I shall have further information for you. Until then, be what you've always been – ready for anything.' He turned aside and nodded at Cameron. 'All right, Number One, carry on, please.'

Cameron saluted and dismissed the hands. There was a buzz of conversation as they dispersed about their part-of-ship duties. Guesses were not hard to make; there had been all that guff from the BBC about Monty's push. The Navy was going to add its weight, maybe mount a bombardment from seaward. The buffer had a quiet word with the leading telegraphist but got no joy there: everything had come through in cypher, and cypher was for officers. But at six o'clock that evening, as the *Oleander* and her charges made their northing through a flat sea, ears were avid for the news broadcast from London. Monty, it seemed, was doing fine. Six days earlier his Desert Rats had come out from their sand-holes and mounted their heavy assault following upon the most devastating artillery barrage that had yet been seen. A sustained pounding over a long front by the big gun-batteries had softened up Rommel's Afrika Corps remarkably, and from El Alamein Monty was pushing steadily west with the intention of driving Rommel into the sea from Cape Bon in Tunisia. There was a long way yet to go but no one aboard the *Oleander* doubted that Monty's infantry and armour would make it.

In the early hours of 2 November the ships moved into the U-boat zone as indicated by the Admiralty's cypher.

In surface action Perry-Grant was action OOW, but since he was also Anti-Submarine Officer the midshipman, Kollenborne, deputized for him on such occasions as this where they knew they were steaming into the U-boat packs. Cameron, having nothing else to do until the fun started, returned to the bridge after checking round the ship above and below. Perry-Grant was half on the bridge, half buried in his Asdic cabinet. It was a crowded bridge, giving Forrest little room to move his big frame. Listening to the monotonous *ping . . . ping* from the Asdic as it swept beneath the sea, Forrest found himself, not for the first time, comparing his present cramped situation with the much more spacious cargo liner in which, before the war, he had been Chief Officer. The old *SS Coverdale* had given a watchkeeper space to move, to walk up and down so as to keep awake during the long night watches. There were few oceans John Forrest had not sailed in his years at sea, few deep-sea ports that he hadn't entered, from Liverpool or the Clyde to Singapore and Penang, Bombay and Calcutta, Sydney and Wellington, New York, San Francisco and Shanghai. He was steeped in the sea and ships, had a good deal more sea-time and navigational experience behind him than any RN officer of his rank. This he knew, though he didn't make his knowledge obvious. He was aware of his own shortcomings *vis-à-vis* the RN: his knowledge of gunnery was rudimentary, obtained during a crash course at the Devonport Gunnery School soon after mobilization; of torpedoes he knew nothing and any RN officer specializing in signals would have left him a non-starter in reading off a flag hoist; he had not been steeped in RN routine and tradition from his earliest years. He had had a lot to learn in a short time and now he had got as far as he was going to go in wartime: as a temporary RNR, one who had not joined the reserve in peacetime, he would never get a brass hat as Commander. Nevertheless, he was content enough. The end of the war would take him back to the Merchant Service and possibly a command; in the meantime he had a good ship and a good ship's company.

However, he was far from sure about Perry-Grant. He tended to distrust lawyers so maybe he was being unfair. He would have to watch that. Four years earlier he had spent a lot of hard-earned money on lawyers, going through the harrowing experience of a divorce. Lawyers were a shifty bunch, always dreaming up some new expense, and they'd made rings round him. If only they had had a till, like a grocer, you could keep a check on what you were spending but when the lengthy reckoning came in it was impossible to sift the wheat from the chaff. . . .

His mind came back suddenly to the present: the note of the Asdic had changed. Perry-Grant had tensed up.

'What is it?' Forrest asked. 'A contact?'

'I think so,' Perry-Grant answered. 'The evidence suggests – '

'Bugger the evidence,' Forrest snapped, 'let's have the bearing.'

Perry-Grant said, 'Red four-five, sir.' He paused, waiting for the Asdic operator. The rating looked round, clamping his ear-phones tighter, and nodded. Perry-Grant said, 'Contact, sir, positive.'

'Right,' Forrest said grimly. 'Keep on it. Warn the depth charges.' He turned to Kollenborne. 'Port ten, maximum revolutions.'

'Port ten, sir, maximum revolutions.' Kollenborne passed the order down.

'Steady!'

'Steady, sir.'

Forrest lifted the sound-powered telephone and spoke to the engine-room. 'Contact, Chief. Attacking.' He put the phone back on its hook and spoke to the leading signalman. 'Warn the *Wiltshire,* and the rest of the escort. Blue-shaded

Aldis.'

'Aye, aye, sir.' At once the dimmed lamp began clacking out its message. The *Oleander* forged ahead at something over her official maximum of sixteen knots. Sixteen knots was a rotten speed, Forrest thought, and they would never have been chosen for the escort of the *Wiltshire* if anything else had been available. The *Mars* was a different story: slow and solid – but *Wiltshire* would have done better on her own. Meanwhile, as *Oleander* moved out of formation, the big ships were maintaining the zig-zag pattern and *Wiltshire* was directing her course to starboard. The Asdic was pinging away like mad now, an almost continuous high note. The reports came through via Perry-Grant: not far to go. Forrest passed the stand-by to the depth-charge party aft. He was coming up to his firing position when there was a massive explosion off the starboard quarter, a huge reverberation shaking the corvette and making everything ring. Forrest didn't turn his head. He asked, 'What was that, for God's sake?'

Cameron said, 'The *Wiltshire*, sir.'

'Poor buggers. We carry on the attack.' Forrest gave the firing order as the Asdic told him he was over his contact. The corvette raced on as the depth-charge pattern was flung out behind. Seconds ticked away, and the bridge personnel looked aft. The charges went up, great spouts of water rearing over the sea. Shock waves were felt through the ship's hull. The *Wiltshire* was seen to be on fire amidships, and was turning in circles, slowly, as though she had lost power. She flamed like a torch in the night, sending red flickers across the water. Forrest said, 'I'm going in again, Number One. Stand by depth charges.'

The word went aft; already Petty Officer Bowling, non-substantive rate seaman torpedoman first class, had got his depth-charge party sweating their guts out to rig new charges in the throwers. On the bridge the Captain brought his ship back on an attacking course, moving in for what should be the kill if he had made his attacks properly. It was: soon after

16

the second pattern had been fired, a bow was seen to break surface, kicking up a kerfuffle of spray, then the whole U-boat came into sight. She had a drunken list to starboard but seemed otherwise intact: it hadn't been quite a kill after all. Forrest, staring through binoculars, ordered the 4-inch gun's crew to train and open just as the U-boat's surface weapons went into action. Everyone on the corvette's bridge ducked as a shell whined across overhead, expending itself in the sea. Then there was a flash at the base of the U-boat's conning tower, followed closely by another on her fore casing. When the smoke cleared, the watchers from the corvette saw that the conning tower had lifted sideways and a big hole was exposed, a hole filled with flame. Another fire burned along the fore casing. There was no more firing.

Kollenborne asked, 'Do we pick up survivors, sir?'

Forrest gave a laugh; it was a hard, grim sound. 'Not German ones, Mid,' he said. 'Put the ship handy for the poor bloody *Wiltshire.*'

'Me, sir?' Kollenborne seemed astonished.

Again Forrest laughed. 'Yes, you, sir. Let's see what sort of a fist you make at it, shall we?'

By now there were more contacts; contacts all over the place. Two more torpedoes struck the *Wiltshire* and she went up in a series of explosions that shattered her hull. Debris was flung into the skies over a wide area, and burning oil fuel seeped across the water, a monstrous spread of death. The cries of men trapped by the moving furnace was blood-curdling, horrible. The corvette moved in, rescuing what there was to be rescued, scrambling nets lowered along her shallow sides. She moved right into the flames, which licked along her metal and ate paintwork, lifting their searing heat to the men on her decks. On the other side of the space where the cruiser had been, *Forsythia* was assisting in the pick-up. The survivors were few, those who could be brought aboard were less. *Oleander* picked up twenty-three men, most of them very badly burned, some of them minus arms

17

or legs, some of them with stomach wounds, chest wounds, head wounds.

Appalled, Forrest stared down from his bridge. 'No doctor,' he said. 'What the bloody hell can we do for them?'

It was a rhetorical question. The only answer was nothing at all. Just give them somewhere comfortable to die, if comfort wasn't too cruel a word, too cruel a thought even, in the circumstances. Forrest was thinking of the doctors and sick bay aboard the *Mars* when the depot ship was herself struck by what appeared to be three torpedoes simultaneously, and recent history repeated itself. Up to a point: the *Mars* hadn't lost her headway. Ablaze from stem to stern she moved on, steering still and heading towards a surfaced U-boat, lying clearly visible in the moonlight and the terrible conflagration. From the corvette's deck Cameron watched in something like awe. On the high compass platform of the depot ship her Captain could be seen, standing in the fore part, staring for'ard, the fires' light playing around the gold oak-leaves that rimmed his cap. Then the U-boat opened with her gun, and the compass platform and the Captain vanished in a searing white-hot ball of flame. After that, another explosion, something internal, deep down. The ship's side seemed to open outwards, pouring thick smoke. From amid the smoke the tannoy system came alive: something was working yet, the circuit lived on. Cameron heard the urgent voice: 'Abandon ship! All hands muster on the upper deck. Abandon ship. This is the Commander speaking. Good luck to you all.'

Oleander moved in again. The single destroyer of the escort went with her. All told, between the ships of the escort, some three hundred of the survivors from the *Mars* were taken aboard. The time came when it was physically impossible to embark any more and the destroyer's captain signalled *Oleander* that they must now consider the safety of those already taken aboard. Every moment of delay held immense danger. With a heavy heart Forrest put his command ahead for Gibraltar and the escort moved away across the dreadful stretch of water, burning in patches still, reeking of death, pursued for a while by the despairing cries and pleas of wounded men.

They zig-zagged continuously, the destroyer moving around the two slow corvettes like a protecting sheepdog. After dawn Petty Officer Osbaldston made the simile to his winger, Ordinary Seaman Passfield: Osbaldston was a York-shireman – Harrogate, but he'd spent a lot of time as a youngster on a bike or in a bus or walking the fells and dales of the North Riding. He reckoned he knew every inch of country from Ingleborough and its stupendous pothole Gaping Ghyll, right across to the Whitby Moors and the Cleveland Hills and south from Barnard Castle to Wensley-dale. That was sheep country largely and when Osbaldston said to Passfield, 'It's just like t'fell farmers, rounding up t'ewes in t'dales back o' Hawes or Bainbridge,' he knew what he was talking about. 'She'll be around us, like as not, all t'way into Gib.'

Passfield nodded but didn't comment. He knew nothing of Yorkshire in any case; he was a CW candidate, in for a com-mission, and came from Croydon. He'd worked for a firm of estate agents, all town stuff. In any case he was unsure of himself where PO Osbaldston was concerned. He'd been alarmed when soon after he'd joined the corvette, which wasn't long ago, the buffer had come along to where he was working part-of-ship, washing down the fo'c'sle, and asked, in a confidential sort of way, if he, Passfield, would like to be his winger. Passfield, not long in the Navy and aboard his first seagoing ship, hadn't known what 'winger' meant but had had sundry warnings in the past from his father about approaches by older men; and he'd feared the worst. Result, he'd been non-committal. Then he'd sought advice from a three-badge AB, a fossil of forty, who'd laughed like a drain and told him not to be bloody wet, there was nothing like that about the buffer and a winger was just a youngster who looked as though he needed to be taken under someone's wing, put right in general and shown the ropes in a friendly, non-official way. The buffer would be a kind of sea-daddy, to use the Service expression. That was all right, and Passfield had gone along to the buffer and said yes, he'd like to be his winger and thank you very much.

Osbaldston had said gruffly, 'Took your bloody time over it an' all, eh? Never mind, though.' Now, as the corvette made her protected dash for Gibraltar, he said kindly, 'Don't brood on last night, lad. It doesn't happen all the time. Likely we'll see no more of t'sods all t'way in.'

And they didn't; there were no further attacks, no manifestations of the enemy. The W/T office had intercepted a signal in German Naval cypher during the early hours and although this could not be broken down a guess was made by the Captain that it was addressed to the U-boat pack, who would probably surface under cover of the dark to re-charge batteries and take the radio routines. It was anyone's guess as to what that signal contained. So, warily, suspiciously, *Oleander* moved on for Gibraltar; but the lurid night scenes remained with all of them and the sight of the wounded from the cruiser and the depot ship kept them constantly reminded of what they were wishful to forget. So did the many sea burials, conducted by the Captain, when the twisting bodies flopped into the South Atlantic from beneath the folds of the White Ensign, men they had never known, leaving mourning families of whom they knew even less. On the bridge, Forrest was suffering, thinking of what he'd been unable to do for his mutilated passengers; he spent most of his time on the bridge and when possible Cameron stayed with him, ready to talk when required. But Forrest didn't say much; just brooded out over the sea. It had all been a very nasty experience and the sheer size of it had left its mark.

It was not a happy arrival in Gibraltar Bay.

3

They entered at a little after 0730 hours the following day. 'Just look at that,' Forrest said, almost in awe. The inner harbour and the anchorage outside seemed already to be crammed to capacity, yet more ships were entering by the minute. To call it an armada would have been an understatement. On the fo'c'sle, standing by the starboard anchor with Cameron, the buffer remarked that it was the biggest assembly of ships he'd seen since the Coronation Review at Spithead back in 1937.

'And it puts that to shame and all,' he said. He spat on his hands. 'Make bloody Hitler think, will that. Musso, too. Mary nostrum my arse! After this lot, both sods can kiss it.'

On the bridge, the Captain watched for his anchor bearings so as to take up position as signalled from the Tower, the headquarters of the Rear-Admiral, Gibraltar. It was a hazy morning, with just a thin sun behind the haze. Gibraltar in November could be cold, and it was; the ship's company had already shifted into blue uniforms, but still wore white cap covers. They came below the immensity of the Rock, brown and purple above the nestling white buildings of the town. The Rock apart, they were half surrounded by Spain, a hostile neutral, full of those watching German eyes. Behind them to the south, across the Straits, lay the mountains of North Africa. As the green anchor flag, held aloft in the Captain's hand, came down sharply, Cameron dropped his own in response and shouted the order to let go; the anchor rattled out in a cloud of red dust from the cable locker; the ship was brought up at two shackles and as soon as she had got her cable the slips were put on and the cable party was fallen out. Cameron looked again at the great assembly. Assault convoys from the Clyde, from Loch Ewe, from Milford Haven as he knew from his study of TSGO – colliers, tugs, ammunition and store ships, tankers, troopships, vessels carrying cased aircraft and tank landing ships, trawlers, all with their warship escorts. And the covering forces, most impressive of all: the *Rodney* with her personal escort, the aircraft carriers *Victorious* and *Formidable* of Force H plus the *Furious* from the Clyde, another battleship, *HMS Duke of York*, the cruisers *Bermuda, Sirius, Aurora, Norfolk, Cumberland*; destroyers, submarines, headquarters ships, corvettes, anti-submarine trawlers, minesweepers and the vital landing craft that would put the troops ashore – Landing Ships Infantry, Landing Ships Tank, Landing Ships Gantry.

Cameron went to the bridge, met Forrest coming down the ladder. Forrest said, 'It's early, but I've already been bidden ashore. The Tower. Not, I hope, as ominous as it sounds! I'd like you to come with me.'

'Aye, aye, sir.' Cameron hesitated. 'What about the survivors?'

'Hospital launches'll be coming off directly,' Forrest said, and went to his cabin. Cameron cleaned into his best suit of number threes. He changed quickly, and was on deck to meet the hospital launches as they came alongside. A surgeon lieutenant clambered aboard; Cameron made himself known.

'Pretty fair shambles,' the doctor said, 'according to the signal from your Captain.'

'Right, it is. I have to go ashore, but Perry-Grant'll see to anything you want done.' Cameron beckoned up the lieutenant. 'What's the first thing, Doctor?'

'First thing's morphine – my job. Then we'll embark them with your assistance.'

Cameron nodded. 'How are things ashore?'

'Crowded,' the doctor answered with a grin. 'If the Nazis

attacked now, they'd have a field day. Just as well we're a shade too far from the bomber bases.' He went off with Perry-Grant, who was looking white and sick. In the calm serenity of the law courts, there wasn't much blood about.

Forrest made his verbal report to the Chief of Staff, backing it with his official write-up of events on passage. Captain Symons, the Chief of Staff, an RN four-ringer, was grave and ominous, though there was no suggestion that *Oleander* or the other escorts had been in any way to blame. If there was blame it lay elsewhere: the ships should have had a faster and stronger escort. '*Mars* is going to be missed,' Symons said briefly. 'This leaves Algiers a shade naked. We're short of depot ships and there happens to be no replacement available. Anyway, there we are. It's in the past. As to you ... are your requirements being met?'

Forrest nodded. 'Yes, sir, thank you.'

'Right.' The Chief of Staff reached into a drawer of his desk and brought out a sealed envelope bearing, like TSGO, the MOST SECRET classification and marked BY HAND OF OFFICER. This he tapped for a moment on his blotter. 'Orders,' he said. 'For *Oleander,* superseding part of what's laid down in TSGO. These take priority. You'll know already, of course, that you're to join the main assault in the Central Sector. That stands. You'll not open this envelope until you're alongside the mole in Mers-el-Kebir. Understood?'

'Understood, sir.'

Symons got to his feet and held out a hand. 'Then it remains only for me to wish you the best of luck, Captain. It's going to be a bloody show, but when it's successful it'll turn the tide of the war.'

Once outside in the dockyard, Forrest grinned and said, 'I like the use of when instead of if, Number One. That's the great thing about us British, isn't it? We don't suffer much from doubt!'

'Full of bull, sir, that's us. But it pays off in the long run.'

'Yes, that's true,' Forrest said soberly. They walked on past gangs of Spanish dockyard mateys, potential spies in Forrest's opinion, taking back more than nicked perks when they crossed the frontier nightly into their native Spain. 'It didn't pay off for those poor devils back there,' Forrest added, jerking a hand towards the south-west.

Cameron said, 'We have to forget it now.' Forrest, he thought, was brooding too much, seemed in some obscure way to be taking the blame on his own shoulders. Cameron suddenly felt old and experienced beyond his years. Here he was, almost lecturing to a man nearly old enough to be his father, a man who had spent some twenty years at sea, and Forrest didn't appear to be taking any umbrage. Forrest, in fact, was scarcely listening: he was thinking back in time as he strode heavily through the clutter of the dockyard, past the waiting battleships and cruisers, not hearing even the strident notes of the bugles as the ships' companies were called to Divisions on the great quarterdecks of the fleet and the White Ensigns were hoisted to the ensign staffs at the start of yet another day's work. From the *Duke of York* and the *Rodney,* from the aircraft carriers, came the sound of the Royal Marine bands beating out 'God Save the King'. Forrest and Cameron walked on, avoiding rusting machinery and old anchor cables, parts of boats that would never cross the harbour again and piles of rotting rope that could have been left behind by Nelson's ships long ago. Forrest was thinking that he was to blame for quite a number of things: if he hadn't been away so much, steaming across half the world, Jane wouldn't have gone off the rails. The marriage had been happy, idyllic almost in the short spells of leave, until Jane had grown restless.

So many times she'd pleaded with him to leave the sea. A poultry farm, she'd said. A nice little place in the country where they could be together all the time. Her father would help financially until they were on their feet. Forrest wouldn't hear of it. He wasn't going to be dependent on anyone but himself, even by way of a loan. And the sea was his life; he loved it, and wanted to command a ship one fine day. He didn't by any means dislike the country, preferred it to the town in fact, but still didn't see himself mucking out henhouses and going off to market or whatever with baskets of eggs.

But perhaps he'd been selfish. Women did get lonely. All right for the man. A career wasn't the whole of life; he'd been realizing that more and more, even to the extent that he was beginning to doubt his fitness to command. He had to shake himself out of that.

Back aboard, there was trouble. Perry-Grant had made a cruel hash but wasn't going to admit it. One of the cot cases had been dropped, slap on to the canopy of the hospital launch. The man had not been among the worst cases and hadn't been given a pain-killing injection. So many of them had been in urgent need that the Surgeon Lieutenant was having to watch his supply of morphine. The man had been badly shaken up and had now been doped after all; the doctor wouldn't know the damage until he got him ashore to the base hospital.

Forrest, his face tight and angry, said, 'Investigate and report, Number One.'

Cameron did so. A leading seaman named Newcombe had been in charge of a party transferring the wounded across into the launch. There had been, Newcombe said, a cock-up and the Neil Robinson stretcher had taken charge. More than that Cameron couldn't disentangle, but Newcombe looked mightily disgruntled. Perry-Grant's story was a little different: Newcombe wasn't much use as a leading seaman, was unable to take charge properly, and he'd had to intervene himself. Newcombe hadn't liked that and had disobeyed an order and because of that the man had been dropped.

Cameron asked casually, 'What order?'

Perry-Grant flushed and shifted his eyes. 'Oh, I told him the proper way to lower a stretcher, that's all.'

25

'And that was?'

Perry-Grant started to shake. He grew pettish. 'Look it up in the Seamanship Manual,' he snapped. 'If you're so damned efficient, you ought to know for yourself.' He turned away and almost ran along the deck. It was more of a scuttle than a run. For the first time Cameron noticed a tendency to knock knees. He didn't call Perry-Grant back; he didn't wish for a disorderly scene in front of ratings, and he hadn't the gift of the gab, as Perry-Grant had. He could be out-talked. However, he was able to come to a few conclusions and these he presented to the Captain in the latter's cabin.

He said, 'I doubt if it was any fault of Newcombe's. He's a long-service rating and he's had his hook for three years.'

'Yes. A damn good seaman. He'll be coming up for PO shortly.'

Cameron nodded. 'I think that's why he wasn't more forthcoming. When you're due for PO you don't tell tales on officers. Right, sir?'

'Very right, I shouldn't wonder! Another thing: I'd a damn sight rather be lowered into a boat by Newcombe than by Perry-Grant. Grant doesn't know a derrick-whip from a fried egg – but that's between you and me. A bloody lawyer, Number One – he could even make a case of slander out of a bollocking from his Captain, let alone a statement made to a third party!' Forrest fumed for a moment, then went on, 'I'll offer a diagnosis and you can shoot it down if you wish: Grant, and bugger the Perry, has to prove he's an officer. He has to make it obvious, not just be there with a watchful eye open like most of us. So he gives unnecessary orders, interferes, ballses things up. That's what happened this time. In the general kerfuffle, that man got dropped. Agree?'

'It sounds only too likely, sir.'

'Yes. Now I have to decide what to do about it. And this is my decision: no action will be taken against Leading Seaman Newcombe, who's certainly not going to suffer for a bloody idiot. I'll have a few choice words in Mr Grant's ear shortly.'

Tongue in cheek Cameron asked, 'And risk that slander action, sir?'

'Shut up, Number One, and have a gin. It's early but it feels later – and we won't have many more chances.'

Some hours after full dark the assault convoys with their escorts moved out from the harbour and anchorage and took up formation for the last stage, the Central and Eastern Task Forces now on the move, the former towards Oran and Mers-el-Kebir, the latter for the assault on Algiers. *Oleander*, with the Central Task Force, passed abeam of Europa Point a little before midnight, at which time Perry-Grant took over the watch from Cameron. The run to the take-off point for the beaches would take only some seventeen hours at a speed of sixteen knots; the speed of the Eastern Task Force would therefore be reduced once the ships were nicely into the Mediterranean so as to permit an arrival off the final assault positions at 0100 hours on 8 November – twenty-five hours ahead yet. Forrest decided that he would put his ship's company fully in the picture after dawn action stations. Meanwhile he remained on the bridge, aware of animosity issuing from his Officer of the Watch. Too bad! He had let himself go on Perry-Grant and didn't regret it. The man who had been dropped might for all he knew spend a lifetime of suffering as a result, which would be a poor thing to happen to a man who had survived a blowing-up. Perry-Grant had tried to wriggle out from under and had repeated his view that Newcombe wasn't fit to hold his rate. Forrest had said that Perry-Grant wasn't fit to judge, and even Perry-Grant's legal training hadn't enabled him to produce an answer to that one. But he'd been white with anger and had shaken like a leaf throughout his bollocking. He was going to be a useless subordinate henceforward but had to be suffered: Forrest did not intend to bother authority with a request for a replacement when Torch was about to get under way.

In the seamen's messdeck, Leading Seaman Newcombe

was still disgruntled. Nothing more had been said but that wasn't the point. Newcombe had a conscience and he didn't want to go down in history as the bloke who'd dropped an already injured man. Perry-Grant was a nasty little bastard with no chin and an oily manner and from now on he would have it in for Newcombe, who knew all about officers having it in for ratings. It had happened to him before, back in peacetime, when he'd fallen foul of a sub-lieutenant in a cruiser. Subby had fancied he was God – which, to the midshipmen, he was, seeing he was Sub of the Gunroom with the power to cane for real or dreamed-up sins. Not to Able Seaman Newcombe as he then was; Newcombe could lose him in five seconds flat when it came to seamanship. He was pompous and a bleeding liar and like Perry-Grant he'd interfered with those that knew better. Result, one fine day in Rosyth he'd been responsible for a motor-cutter being secured with one rope on the standing part of the jetty and the other on the floating pontoon. The motor-cutter had been left in the charge of a boat-keeper, an ordinary seaman who'd panicked when the tide ebbed, while Subby, Newcombe and an exercise party had doubled in PT gear all round the dockyard. When they got back on the ebbing tide, the motor-cutter was standing on its head and later the cruiser's Commander had gone berserk. Newcombe, partly in protection of the OD left in charge, had told the truth, adding that he'd done his best to impress it on the sub-lieutenant that his ideas were all to buggery. Subby had then landed the blame on Newcombe for wilfully not understanding what he'd said. Newcombe carried the can since the boat was primarily his responsibility and he took his punishment, but the skipper hadn't been daft and Newcombe knew that Subby had been given a prize rocket and had his leave stopped for a month. From then on, Newcombe's life had been hell. It could be so again. *Would* be, in a different sense, when they got to wherever they were going. By this time it was obvious that they were heading for an actual landing on enemy-held territory. The brown jobs would get it first, of course. Americans . . . the transports seemed to be carrying solid phalanxes of Yanks, people whom Newcombe viewed with British sourness. Not in the war five minutes but every man among them covered with gaudy medal ribbons. A decoration for leaving home and mom, Long Service medal for sticking it six weeks, something else for embarking . . . not true, of course. Just British jealousy.

And they were a sight better than Perry-Grant.

Forrest was wondering about those sealed orders, wondering too if he would in fact live to open the envelope. He had a working idea of what lay ahead, so close ahead now. The ships would go in and the landing craft would discharge their troops on the beaches, then go back to the transports for more and more again, a continuous wave of men to be put ashore and move inland; all under a withering fire that would cut into them in swathes of fiery tracer. By this time there could surely be no secrecy left; the Jerries would be massed in strength, a very ready welcoming committee.

It was far from warm but Forrest found himself sticky with sweat; his hands were clammy on the bridge rail as he sat on a high chair staring for'ard above his pipsqueak 4-inch gun, which, manned as for cruising stations, would soon be manned for action.

0400 . . . he heard Perry-Grant's voice, full of complaint. 'Captain, sir. My relief's late.'

'It's only just on four, Grant.

There was an angry, or petulant, intake of breath at the lack of a Perry. 'Yes, sir. But it's customary for one's relief to come up in time to be handed over to before the actual change of watch.'

'I know what's customary.' Forrest's voice was sharp. There was no response from Perry-Grant. Five more minutes passed and then Lightwell came up, breathless and full of apologies.

'It's not good enough,' Perry-Grant said loudly.

Forrest asked, 'Did the boatswain's mate miss you out,

29

Lightwell?'

'Oh no, sir. I'm afraid it was my fault, sir. I woke up, then went to sleep again.'

'I see.' Point in favour: the Sub hadn't tried to slide out of it. 'Bad show, Lightwell. Don't let it happen again.'

'No, sir.'

Forrest believed it wouldn't happen again. Lightwell had proved a fast learner and took rebukes to heart as well. Conscientiousness was his keyword. Forrest leaned forward in his seat, chin resting on the backs of his hands. Behind him Perry-Grant made his hand-over to Lightwell, giving the course and revolutions, still sounding petulant. Forrest heard him start to clatter down the ladder and called him back.

'Grant.'

'Yes, sir?' The footsteps halted.

'Wind – direction and strength. You've not passed it on.'

'Light airs only, sir.'

'Light airs are wind, Grant.'

There was a pause, a silence broken only by the sounds of ship and sea – water hissing along the plates, the hum of dynamos and ventilators, the sounds that sink into the background, into the subconscious of a seaman. Forrest could guess what was passing through the former lawyer's mind: any fool, even Lightwell, should be able to assess the wind for himself. Nevertheless, the routines had to be kept to. They were a vital part of total efficiency. The pause ended when Perry-Grant snapped, 'Shifting, but mainly easterly,' and then went on down the ladder. Forrest turned and looked aft; his wake was streaming astern, like those of the ships ahead and on either beam green with a brilliance of phosphorescent light. The weather was too good. Their way was being unkindly lit, like the other night when the *Wiltshire* and the *Mars* had gone.

Forrest was still on the bridge when the dawn came up, streaking the sky ahead, and the ship went to dawn action stations. He yawned and stretched wearily, then raked the

30

horizons and the sky with his binoculars. Nothing. It was a ruddy miracle, he thought. God must be with them, as the padres always insisted he was, but God could desert them as they made the final approach run to the Oran beaches. God was unlikely to be a Nazi but he might not be an Imperialist either. He could stand aloof.

Soon it was bright day, a brilliant one. Still the ships steamed in Allied solitariness. Forrest, as Cameron came to the bridge, said abruptly, 'All right, Number One. Secure from action stations.'

'Aye, aye, sir. Will you speak to the ship's company now, sir?'

'I was about to say that very thing. Pipe 'em to muster, Number One.'

Cameron passed the order. From the wheelhouse the boatswain's mate of the watch made his way below and piped around the ship. 'Fall out action stations, all hands off watch to muster on the fo'c'sle . . .'

When Cameron had reported the hands mustered, Forrest stood up and leaned over the fore rail of the bridge. He said, 'The air's been as full of buzzes as a dog of fleas and I more than suspect you've all tumbled to the facts. Am I right?'

There was laughter and some confused talk. They'd tumbled, all right. For form's sake, Forrest confirmed it. 'We're going in to back up General Montgomery and the Eighth Army and drive the Nazis . . .' His voice tailed off as the cheering started. He let it go for a while; they were letting off steam, enjoying themselves, raring to go – they might change that effervesence before much longer. Let them show it for now. Then he held up his hand and went on.

'I don't need to stress the size of it all. This convoy's only a part. We ourselves are under orders to reach a point off Oran in Algeria, where the Central Task Force will establish three beachheads, two of them a little to the westward of the naval port of Mers-el-Kebir, the third one eastwards of Oran in the vicinity of Cape Carbon. This eastern assault will be the biggest of the three – 29,000 men, 2,400 vehicles including tanks, around 15,000 tons of stores involving thirty-four merchant ships, plus a large number of landing craft, and plus the warships involved. *Oleander* will detach earlier and when we get the executive from the covering force, we shall enter Mers-el-Kebir. *Forsythia* and one destroyer, the *Halberdier,* will be in company.' Forrest paused. 'I'm making the assumption the general idea is simply to create a diversion, since in fact Mers-el-Kebir is not to come under actual attack by the landing force. I expect you all know what that means.'

They knew, all right. Forrest hadn't much more to say after that, and when he had finished Cameron dismissed the hands. Talking to the coxswain as they went aft, Osbaldston said, 'Draw the buggers' fire, eh, 'swain?'

The coxswain, Chief Petty Officer Hampson, nodded. 'We're the fall guys, Buff, as the Yanks say. And God help us, that's all I can say. I know some who won't.' As he said the words, he was staring directly at the depth-charge throwers, where Perry-Grant happened to be standing.

4

THAT day passed with a semblance of normality but the tension was evident along the messdecks, at the guns, on the bridge and in the wardroom. Tension was also, if for different reasons, being felt in the small compartment used as the Captain's office, which was Midshipman Kollenborne's occasional kingdom. In between his upper deck duties, Kollenborne acted as correspondence officer, dealing with official letters and all the many forms required by such authorities as the Board of Admiralty and the Director of Navy Accounts to be filled in at frequent intervals. Midshipman Kollenborne stood out a mile aboard the corvette because of the white patches on the lapels of his blue uniform jacket which indicated that he was RN, the only regular officer in the ship. He was a fish out of water and to some extent had been so from his earliest Dartmouth days. His father was an estate agent and the Navy, still exclusive in its social backgrounds, had not yet got around to thinking very highly of estate agents. Most of Kollenborne's contemporaries seemed to be the offspring of service officers, largely naval, with a fair sprinkling of very senior ranks. Those who were not were the sons of genuine professional men, doctors, solicitors and so on or just plain landed gentry or members of parliament – or so it had seemed and still seemed to Midshipman Kollenborne. He had become ultra-sensitive on parentage, carrying an obsession to ridiculous lengths. His youthful contemporaries were inclined to regard estate agents as erks who – in the cases of those whose fathers were RN – sent out lists of unsuitable furnished flats in Southsea, Plymouth and the Medway towns, the usual homes of not-very-well-paid naval officers. So Kollenborne tended not to mention estate agents. Today he was almost forced to when he was visited by Ordinary Seaman Passfield. Kollenborne's duties as correspondence officer included the care of the ratings' 'parchments' or service certificates, documents that indicated their owners' civilian occupations; and Kollenborne was aware that Passfield had been an assistant in an estate agency. That morning, the last before action was due to commence, Kollenborne was completing a return concerned with the supply of beef. Records had to be kept up to date even though all hands might be dead within the next twenty-four hours. The midshipman was about to turn his attention to his next chore when Passfield tapped at the door: Ordinary Seaman Passfield, candidate for an RNVR commission, looking nervous, as though even so lowly a representative of the straight-stripe RN as a midshipman might bite.

'Yes?' Kollenborne asked.

'Sorry to bother you, sir.'

'That's all right. What is it?'

'The mail, sir. I've written a letter home.'

'You should have posted it in Gib.'

'It wasn't written then, sir. It was an afterthought. I was wondering when the next mail would be landed?'

Kollenborne laughed rather edgily. 'God, how should I know? Depends whether we capture Oran or not, I suppose! You'll be told, all in good time, don't worry.'

'Yes, sir. I suppose I'm not the only one who's written home since we left Gibraltar.' Still in the doorway, Passfield hesitated. He seemed to have something else to say. Kollenborne, who was a kindly enough person, grinned and asked if there was anything he could do. He rather hoped there wasn't; Passfield had a nasty rash around his face, especially the chin, and on his neck. It could be just a shaving rash, but on the other hand it could be impetigo. Very catching. Kollenborne was well up in the study of medical dictionaries and

34

liked to stand clear of infection.

Passfield said, 'Well, sir, as a matter of fact I've been meaning to ask you, if you didn't think it cheek.' He gave an embarrassed cough. 'Your name, sir. It's an unusual one. My firm – I worked for some estate agents – they used to do business with a firm called Kollenborne and Pratt, in Oxford – '

'Oh, really?' The tone was distant, not to say chilling.

'Yes. My firm was in Croydon as it happens, but they had connections in – '

'I'm awfully sorry, old chap,' Kollenborne broke in, his face suddenly as red as a beetroot. 'I've got to get some returns finished for the Captain to sign. I thought perhaps you wanted something sort of official. You don't mind, do you?'

'Of course not, sir,' Passfield said at once, but had a hurt look as he turned away. And a surprised one too: the midshipman had been rattled, it was easy to see that. Really upset, shying like a horse. In the Captain's office Kollenborne sat staring at nothing, fists clenched. Passfield wouldn't be put off for ever. Probably thought a shared interest might lead to help in getting his commission. Soon it would be all round the ship. Lucky there weren't any other RN officers ... Kollenborne's mind went back to RNC Dartmouth, to which he'd gone at the regulation age of thirteen and a half. They'd been as beastly as any other public schoolboys. The hurtful memories lingered and wouldn't die. The captains' sons, the admirals' sons, the under-secretaries of state's sons, had taunted him: Kollenborne's father goes round on a push-bike collecting rent ... Kollenborne's old man gets tipped when he shows people round ... Jew-boy Kollenborne. It had been hateful and it had gone on for a long time. Kollenborne was seeing through a red mist; he seized the beef return and screwed it up, face as crumpled as the piece of paper. It wasn't fair. But – really – did it matter when all hell was due to be let loose next day? Kollenborne said, 'Oh, *shit*,' and tried to straighten out the

35

beef return. It was going to be difficult to explain to Father, when he came to sign it, why it was looking like a piece of bog paper.

Now it was 2200 hours and a dark night. The ship had been some while at action stations. At 1815 the Central Task Force had split in accordance with TSGO. The ships detailed for the western beaches had altered to the south-south-west and by 2315 were due to arrive off their target areas. Some of the groups detailed for the eastern assault on the vicinity of Cape Carbon altered to the south-east. *Oleander* herself, with *Forsythia* and *Halberdier*, had maintained her course until 1950 when she also had altered south-eastwards.

'One hour,' Forrest said. 'One hour to rendezvous with Groups Six and Seven.'

Cameron said, 'Yes, sir.' They knew it all by heart; the Captain was talking just to avoid the silence. At the same time as *Oleander* was given the executive order to detach for Mers-el-Kebir, two former United States coastguard cutters, *Walney* and *Hartland*, would also detach and make at speed for the harbour at Oran, covered by two motor-launches that would make smoke and by the guns of the cruiser *Aurora*; their orders were to burst through the boom and land American troops who were to take all key positions and watch for sabotage. After that, the rest of the ships would move on south-south-easterly, joined now by two more groups of the Task Force, and at 0100 they would be in position to begin putting the troops and armour ashore.

'What are you thinking about, Number One?' Forrest's question was sudden and unexpected.

Cameron gave an honest answer. 'Nothing except pure funk!'

'Same here!' Forrest laughed. 'That, and a very pious hope there's not going to be a colossal balls-up. You know how these things can go.'

'Yes, sir.'

'You've checked everything?'

'Yes, sir. Guns, ready-use ammunition, magazines, depth charges, boats and rafts, main and secondary steering – the lot. All correct, sir. All on the top line.'

'Do it again,' Forrest said abruptly.

'Aye, aye, sir.' Cameron left the bridge. The Captain was right; things could go wrong at awkward moments, without any warning, and you needed to check right up to the last. Cameron made a thorough job of it, going round the ship with the buffer, the coxswain and an ERA. The latter was a thin, earnest man named Lott, first-class at his job, not so good with his hobby, which was women. Many a woman had been known, on a temporary basis, as Lot's wife to his messmates and all had turned out to be pillars of salt – anyway, frigid. Just his bloody rotten luck. Life had soured him as a result and now he scarcely ever bothered to go ashore; he concentrated on the pin-ups wherever they could be found. The petty officers' mess bulkheads were covered with them, to the disgust of the coxswain, who was a man of moral outlook. He considered that Lott should get himself married, settle down and grow up. But pillars of salt had put Lott off the idea; he would probably be unlucky again and saddled with it for life. He seemed to attract frigidity. And Jimmy, as from time immemorial the lower deck had known any First Lieutenant, seemed to know all about it too.

'How's the gallery, Lott?' Cameron asked as they left the tiller flat.

'Fair to middling, sir. Got too much on for my liking,' he added with a sneaking glance at the coxswain, who pursed his lips.

'What happens to them in action?'

Lott lifted his cap and scratched his head, reflectively. 'Dunno, sir. They keeps themselves to themselves, I reckon.' He added, 'With any luck a projy might blow off a few pairs o' knickers.'

The coxswain said witheringly, 'Some people!' The round of inspection proceeded. Lott followed on, frowning. Jimmy had touched a raw spot; he would hate to part company with his collection and never mind that they weren't nude enough. It would be just his luck if Monty came aboard in Oran with all his talk about hitting them for six and leading a clean life so as to be fit to beat the Hun, and poked his skinny, moralizing nose into the mess. Monty was never backward in coming forward, so they said, and he'd have words with the skipper. Monty was a misogynist and probably frigid himself.

Lott went back to the engine-room and Cameron climbed again to the bridge and reported. The tension was mounting fast. The dim shapes in the night, very efficiently blacked out, lumbered on. Cargo-vessels, troopships, warships big and small, all soon likely to be lit up by the thunder of the guns. Forrest moved restlessly, hunching his heavy shoulders, easing the steel helmet that was now upon his head with his stripes of rank painted on the back and front: everyone had to be able to recognize the Captain when the show started.

Suddenly he said, 'Shakespeare had it right. He forecast this lot – that speech in what was it, one of the Henrys.'

Cameron was surprised. 'You read Shakespeare, sir?'

'I'm not illiterate,' Forrest said. 'You know the bit about gentlemen in England, now abed, shall wish like bloody hell they'd been here – something like that?'

It was Perry-Grant who put him right. '"And gentlemen in England, now abed, shall think themselves accursed they were not here, to fight with us upon St Crispin's Day." *Henry V*. The reference being to Agincourt, sir.'

Forrest grunted irritably. He said, 'You've a good voice, I'll say that for you. Wring the heart of any jury.' He stared into the night, feeling a stir in his guts. He believed this was to rank in history as high as any Agincourt or Waterloo but frankly he would have preferred to be abed, he told himself. Yet that wasn't entirely true. He wouldn't have wanted to hang back; the Nazis had to be got rid of, their poison drained out of the system. North Africa had to be purged of Rommel. It wouldn't be an end but it would be the beginning of the end, that he felt in his bones. One massive defeat would shake the Fatherland to its foundations, they would never be the same again. A lot of Hitler's bombast would go for a burton though no doubt he would rant and rave as before. After North Africa, perhaps Italy, with British and American troops putting the bayonet up the bottom of the man Churchill (wasn't it? He wouldn't ask Perry-Grant) had called the bullfrog of the Pontine Marshes.

Perry-Grant spoke again: he was the ship's navigator for good or ill, and, surprisingly, not at all bad. 'Coming into position, sir.'

'Thank you. We maintain course and speed. I see Groups Six and Seven coming up, or I think I do.' Forrest busied himself with his binoculars and a moment after, somewhat late, the port bridge lookout reported the leading ships of the converging columns. Forrest said, 'It's your job to see them before me. Keep alert tonight of all nights.'

'Aye, aye, sir.'

Behind the Captain the leading signalman said, 'Blue lamp flashing, sir, from *Aurora*.'

'Us?'

'Yes, sir. Reading, sir.' There was a pause, then the leading signalman said, 'Detaching orders, sir. We're to join *Forsythia* and *Halberdier* on the executive.'

'Right.'

Forrest's hands gripped the bridge rail like vices. At his side Cameron felt his guts turn to water. Within a minute of the warning signal, the executive came from the *Aurora*. Forrest said, 'Right, Number One, this is it. Starboard ten, maximum revolutions,' he added to the OOW.

Perry-Grant repeated the order down the voice-pipe. 'Starboard ten, maximum revolutions.'

The acknowledgement from the coxswain, on the wheel at action stations, came up hollowly. 'Starboard ten, sir, maximum revolutions. Ten of starboard wheel on, sir.'

Forrest was watching the ship's head, watching *Forsythia* and *Halberdier* as they altered course in company for Mers-el-Kebir. 'Midships.'

'Midships, sir. Wheel's amidships, sir.'

'Steady.'

'Steady, sir. Course, two-six-eight degrees, sir.'

'Steer two-seven-two.'

'Two-seven-two, sir.' Then a moment later: 'Course, two-seven-two, sir.'

It was all normal, all routine, the giving and repetition of helm orders. It could be just an ordinary convoy or a welcome return to port after yet another escort run. There was something comforting about the familiarity of naval routine, the sound of friendly voices, the sure knowledge that no one was going to let you down. Other comfort lay in the background to seaward: some twenty-five miles off Oran lay the *Rodney* with three aircraft carriers together with *HMS Delhi*, an anti-aircraft cruiser. Cameron glanced astern: the assault columns had now closed a submarine, *HMS Ursula*, which was lying on the surface as a kind of marker buoy to guide the eastern force. *Halberdier* moved ahead of the two corvettes; *Oleander* was now in the middle, with *Forsythia* astern. *Aurora*, together with the motor-launches that would make smoke, moved into position to give cover to the *Walney* and the *Hartland* as they began their dash to burst through the boom across the entrance to Oran harbour. Cameron saw the cruiser's guns weaving in the turrets as the crews went through the final checks of the firing circuits.

In the wheelhouse the coxswain watched his steering compass phlegmatically. It was quiet, he thought – too quiet by half. It was as though the Jerries were just lying in wait, which they probably were, knowing all the secret orders. The command would be like they gave the infantry: wait till you see the whites of their eyes. Soon the ships would be a lovely target, and never mind the smoke-screen accorded *Walney* and *Hartland*, that would be just eyewash in Chief Petty Officer Hampson's view. Smoke screens were all very well, but they were susceptible to the wind direction, not that there was any wind just at the moment but it could come at the wrong time. Some did in the very instant that Hampson thought about it: Ordinary Seaman Passfield, boatswain's mate of the watch, gave an involuntary belch and Hampson's taut nerves made him react.

'For Christ's sake!'

'Sorry, Chief.'

'Don't bloody do that again. Like a bloody Oerlikon opening up.'

Passfield grinned; the coxswain was all right if short-tempered at times and Passfield was glad his action station kept him close to what he regarded as a tower of strength. Meanwhile the tower of strength's face was bleak: he didn't happen to like Passfield and he knew why, and knew it was unfair and that he had to keep it down. Passfield, spots and all, just happened to look like a little sod called Ken Ricketts, who considered himself to be Hampson's daughter's 'young man'. Ricketts had slid out of the war by being in a reserved occupation and had slid into Hampson's life thereby: he was handy, available every night unlike the more manly ones who'd joined up. Whenever CPO Hampson was on leave, which was seldom enough in all con-science and there had been none since he'd joined *Oleander* on the West Africa station, Ricketts had been there, swanning around the parlour and necking with Dorothy whenever he thought mum and dad weren't around. Ricketts called Hampson Dad, which was cheek seeing as he'd cer-tainly not been invited to do so and it showed a presumption, too soon, of proprietorial rights over Dorothy. They would marry only over Hampson's dead body, not a nice thought tonight. It was Dad this, Dad that, when it was only too obvious that what Ricketts really wanted to say was silly old codger. It was the worse for the fact that Hampson's only son had joined the Navy just before war broke out and had been lost in the Med, blown up in the battleship *Barham* not so far north-east of where Hampson was tonight. Hampson's heart ached just to think of Ricketts in the home where Harry used to be. He must force himself not to take it out on Passfield.

'Port ten.'

The skipper himself, who'd taken over now they were close, and was putting the ship onto her final run in. 'Port ten, sir,' Hampson called up the voice-pipe. 'Ten of port wheel on, sir.'

'Steady.'

'Steady, sir. Course, one-eight-oh, sir.'

It was the routine again; Hampson felt it the same as Forrest. Wrapped in bullshit, you couldn't go under. It was a nice safe net. Didn't always work, of course ... Hampson lifted his head again as the Captain's voice came down once more.

'Cox'n?'

'Sir?'

'About ten minutes to go by my reckoning. I'll let you know when we're through into the harbour.'

'That's if the Jerries don't, sir.'

There was a quiet laugh, nothing further. Hampson appreciated the skipper's gesture, his concern. With the deadlights screwed down over the ports to keep out shell splinters and that, you could see bugger all from the wheel-house. It was nice to know where you were; some skippers didn't bother. Some skippers were like ice and thought you were dirt, especially in the big ships. Not Lieutenant-Commander Forrest; there was more humanity about RNR officers. The approach was more direct, and that could be because in the merchantmen the officers weren't cocooned in King's Regulations, the Articles of War, and the Naval Discipline Act. Discipline, and it existed right enough, had to be enforced by personality rather than rely for back-up on bits of paper and threats. That was what CPO Hampson called leadership. It was something this skipper had for sure.

'All right, Passfield?'

Passfield looked surprised. 'Yes, Chief, I'm all right.'

'Good lad. Got a fag, have you? Left mine in the mess.'

'Yes, Chief,' Passfield produced a packet of Senior

Service. He handed it to the coxswain, with one fag sticking out. He flicked a lighter. Hampson drew smoke in deep, still watching the steering compass closely. The corvette moved on, water hissing down her sides. Hampson sucked at the cigarette like a baby at the breast. It might be the last he'd ever had. He'd just chucked the dog-end into the spitkid on the deck when from outside came a din like the world disintegrating on its last day.

The bridge was lit by red fire: everything stood out stark as an inferno. *Halberdier* had burst through into the harbour, *Oleander* and *Forsythia* following close astern. The destroyer had moved into an intense barrage of fire, a concentration both from the shore and from two small warships in the port, now outlined in the gun-flashes.

Forrest said, '*Halberdier*'s out of control, Number One.' He leaned over the bridge rail and shouted down to the 4-inch HA gun's crew. 'Lightwell!'

The Sub-Lieutenant looked up, all but unrecognizable in his steel helmet and white anti-flash gear. Forrest called out, 'Use the flashes from the shore batteries as your point of aim – open fire!'

'Aye, aye, sir!'

Within moments the 4-inch was in action, its sharp crack making Perry-Grant cover his ears with his hands. There was immense confusion ahead and it was impossible to spot the fall of shot. Now the barrage was shifting on to *Oleander* herself as she came through into the port; but not before *Halberdier* was seen to be on fire and milling around in circles. Now and again it was possible to hear the thunder of more distant gunfire, while some five miles to the eastward the sky over Oran was lit by constant explosions: *Walney* and *Hartland* were having no easy passage inwards, it seemed. Forrest's voice came to Cameron through the appalling din: 'Where the hell's the *Aurora*?'

'I think she's engaged to the north, sir.'

'What?' Forrest swung his glasses. There was a fight of

some kind going on. As he looked the sound-powered telephone buzzed and Cameron picked it up. It was the W/T
office. Cameron took the message and reported to the
Captain.

'Signal on port wave from *Aurora*, sir. She's intercepted
some Vichy destroyers.'

Forrest lowered his glasses. 'French bastards. No wonder
some of our longer-memoried generals in the last war had to
be reminded they were no longer the enemy.' He paused,
seemed about to go on when he staggered across the bridge,
fetching up in a heap with Cameron and Perry-Grant. Something had taken them, slap below the bridge, Forrest
believed. Cursing, he heaved himself to his feet. The leading
signalman, who had been in the starboard bridge-wing, was
draped like his own shroud over his signalling projector,
pouring blood. Forrest grabbed the wheelhouse voice-pipe
and called down for the coxswain.

A shaking voice answered, 'Wheelhouse, sir.'

'Who's that?'

'Ordinary Seaman Passfield, sir.'

'The cox'n – '

'Dead, sir. There's not much left of him. He's – '

'All right, Passfield. Who else is there?'

'Only me, sir. The messenger and telegraphsman are dead
too – '

'Are you fit enough to take the wheel?'

'I – I think I am, sir, yes – '

'Do your best, then. What's the wheelhouse like?' Forrest
feared there could be fire.

'All right, sir. The shell didn't go off, sir . . . it went right
through the port bulkhead.'

And hit the sea, Forrest supposed. Once again he said,
'Do your best, Passfield. Course, still one-eight-oh. I'll be
passing a number of helm orders, so keep your ears
flapping.'

'Aye, aye, sir.'

As the explosions continued all around Forrest had a

useless thought: he'd not kept his promise to the coxswain; he'd been too busy seeing to his command to think about anything else. The fire was murderous; heavy stuff, small arms, close-range weapons, machine guns; endless streams of tracer crisis-crossed the harbour, making patterns of streaking red light. The din-beat at the eardrums. The final outcome, as Forrest remarked, looked less hopeful now. A moment later, there was a vast explosion from astern: *Forsythia* had been hit in a vital spot, probably her magazine, and had blown sky-high. Debris rattled down over *Oleander*'s decks, already raked by the heavy fire. Forrest turned his ship and moved in over the spot where *Forsythia* had been, his ship's company fighting to get the scrambling nets over the sides. Forrest learned later that there were only fifteen survivors from the corvette. As his ship moved on, ably steered to Forrest's orders by Ordinary Seaman Passfield, she came under even more intense fire. From all round them the guns opened up, everything in the port being brought to bear on the only two ships left to carry on the fight. There were casualties along the decks: the gunlayer of the 4-inch was almost sliced in half by a big splinter, a jag of metal ripped from the fore bulkhead of the wheelhouse by a French shell that, like the earlier one, failed to explode on impact. Cameron, looking over the bridge screen, saw the shell lying in the scuppers. No time wasted, he went down the port ladder on the palms of his hands, ran for the projectile and scooped it up.

He threw it over the side.

Going back to the bridge, he found Perry-Grant huddled in the lee of the big signalling projector where the leading signalman had died: the body had fallen to the deck below some while earlier. 'What's up?' he asked.

Perry-Grant was shaking like a leaf. 'Nothing,' he said. Then he added, 'I . . . I don't feel at all well.'

'Better feel well again before Father sees you,' Cameron said, and moved to join the Captain in the fore part of the bridge. Behind him Perry-Grant let out a high sound like a whimper and scuttled for the port ladder. He went down fast, seeking safety: anywhere was better than the bridge or the upper-deck. He went past a decapitated body. Limbs trembling, he went aft almost blindly. He was stopped by a big body and a ham-like fist. He looked up into the furious face of Leading Seaman Newcombe. He said, 'Let me go, Newcombe.'

'Well, if it isn't Mister bloody Perry-Grant. Navvy, aren't you, eh?'

'Yes – '

'Navigator's action station's on the bridge. Bloody skulker. Bloody shit scared – right? Bloody little ponce. Get back up there pronto or I'll shout for Jimmy or the skipper.'

'Let me go. That's an order.' The voice was high, breaking.

'Order my arse. Fuckin' off in action, that's a court martial offence. Dismissal with disgrace. Or death, maybe, I dunno. Get back on the bridge or you've bloody had it, mate. And another thing. One word about what I've just said and I'll have you. In case you haven't bloody noticed, we've got witnesses.'

Perry-Grant, as tracer whipped across above his head, looked upwards. He'd been stopped right below the pom-pom platform. A voice came down to him. 'That's right, what the killick says.'

Tears running down his face, Perry-Grant turned and went back to the bridge. He had, after all, a little pride.

The *Halberdier* had blown up, hit presumably in one of her magazines. She had been carrying a number of American troops, and now the waters of the harbour seemed solid with bodies, British, American and Vichy French. *Oleander* altered westward and continued to fight through alone towards the long arm of the mole in accordance with her orders. By this time *Aurora* was seen outside the break-water, standing off to their assistance, firing her main armament point blank and at close range into the French batteries; in the overall glare her silhouette stood out sharply. She signalled that she had despatched the Vichy destroyers. Now she drew off much of the fire. So far as ship-damage went, *Oleander* had been lucky: after the first two shells she hadn't been hit by anything heavier than the close-range weapons from the French warships in the port. She was under full command and was now approaching the mole that extended from beneath the French Foreign Legion fortress; the firing was falling away as *Aurora*'s guns continued their bombardment. The two enemy warships were seen to blow up and disintegrate in a shatter of metal. Nothing came from ahead as the berthing party was piped to stand by the starboard side; but Forrest was wary of the looming fort and its guns even though they had not joined in the earlier barrage against the British ships. Nevertheless, he said, 'I'm not going to be the first to open, Number One.'

'There's some safety in being the first to react, sir.'

'With popguns?' Forrest gave a grim laugh and wiped sweat from his face. But what I'm getting at is this: not all the French around here are necessarily Vichy. Let's give 'em a chance – a chance to take *their* chance if you follow.'

'Those loyal to de Gaulle might take over, you mean?'

Forrest nodded. They moved on in comparative quiet, through the eerie darkness, coming under the lee of the mole. From the distance came the sound of heavy gunfire, ominous, threatening. Going down to the upper deck for bearthing, Cameron had a feeling the operation was in jeopardy. The swift reaction to their own entry didn't speak too well for the main assault beachheads.

Gently, *Oleander* came alongside the mole.

5

'So here we are, just to coin a phrase,' Forrest said. He looked down from the bridge; the mole appeared deserted and the sudden quiet was unnerving. It had to be a false calm. Forrest added, 'We drew their fire all right, but I wonder to what end? To me, it has all the atmosphere of a damp squib. Why are they holding off now?' The question was rhetorical; Perry-Grant didn't comment. He was simply glad to be alive so far. He looked around: he couldn't see much but knew from the chart that he was enclosed by mountains, hostile mountains holding God knew how many Nazi divisions. Somewhere in the darkness stood Fort Mers-el-Kebir, maybe a mile distant at the landward end of the long mole. As the Captain turned away from the bridge rail, Cameron came up the ladder and reported.

'Ship secured alongside, sir.'

'Thank you, Number One.' Forrest took a deep breath. 'What a bloody shambles! I had a feeling deep down it'd all get ballsed up. Too much planning doesn't always achieve the desired result. Have you had a chance to assess casualties yet?'

Cameron nodded. 'Yes, sir. Six killled, nineteen wounded, eight of them seriously.'

'And once again, no doctor.'

'No. Lightwell's bought it, sir.'

Forrest's head jerked up. 'Dead?'

'I'm afraid so.'

Forrest swore luridly. 'Poor bloody kid. He wasn't much more and never mind Cambridge. How I loathe Nazis.' His hands were clenched tight; through the dark night Cameron could see the knuckles standing out white as the Captain gripped the binoculars slung from his neck on a length of codline. 'The others, Number One?'

'The leading supply assistant, the gunlayer of the 4-inch, the coxswain, Able Seaman Stannard from the close-range weapons aft, and Palfrey, sir.'

Forrest showed his nerves by an edgy laugh; far from a humorous one, far from unfeeling. He said, 'No more over-pink lunch-time gin.' Palfrey had been the wardroom steward, and had an unreliable hand with the Angostura bitters. No amount of complaint had ever had the slightest effect on Palfrey. In civilian life he had been under-butler to a lord who liked plenty of bitters and that was that. Forrest gave himself a shake, trying to clear his mind for a job that had really only just begun. He remembered the orders locked in his safe, the sealed orders handed to him by the Chief of Staff in Gibraltar. He was about to go down and get them himself when Cameron said, 'Someone on the mole, sir. Hear it?'

Forrest listened: someone was there all right, someone coming along at the double. 'Go aft, Number One,' Forrest said. 'Take a revolver. Get Osbaldston to issue rifles.'

'I think it's just one man, sir.'

'Could be more where he came from. Off you go, pronto.'

'Aye, aye, sir.' Cameron slid down the ladder, calling for Petty Officer Osbaldston who materialized from the close-range weapons aft of the bridge. Cameron passed the orders and ran on aft to the quarterdeck. The mole seemed to extend to infinity; sound was carrying in the otherwise strangely silent night though the darkness was thick and Cameron couldn't yet see the runner. He waited, feeling the reaction in his guts.

Osbaldston came back with four seamen, all armed and with bayonets already fixed. 'Just in case like, sir,' Osbaldston said. He said it with a certain satisfaction; he would very much like, that night after his friend CPO Hampson had died, to shove some shining steel up Vichy French backsides, or Nazi ones if that was how the cookie was to crumble as the Yanks had it.

The running footsteps came nearer. A figure, dimly seen now, halted alongside the corvette. Osbaldston said, 'I believe he's a Frog, sir. He has that sort of look, I reckon. Open fire on the bugger, sir?'

'For God's sake, no – '

'Put a torch on him, then, sir?'

'Yes, all right. Watch it, you men,' Cameron added to the armed party behind him. The buffer flicked on a pocket torch, played the beam on the solitary man. He was French right enough; cavalry greatcoat, brown leather knee-boots, *bourguignotte* helmet of manganese steel, French officer's badges of rank. Cameron called across, 'Who are you?'

'Henri de Beaufois, *capitaine* in the Foreign Legion of France, from Mers-el-Kebir.' There was a pause. '*Vive de Gaulle! Vive l'honneur de la France!*'

'And kiss my arse,' Osbaldston muttered sourly. 'How do we know he's not giving us a load of codswallop, sir?'

'We'll have to chance it,' Cameron said. 'He's alone and can't do much harm.' He raised his voice towards the mole. 'What do you want, Captain?'

'To speak to the *Capitaine* of your ship. My Colonel asks British assistance to guard the mole.'

'Against whom?'

'The *Petainistes*, the Vichy. My Colonel has taken the fort for Generale de Gaulle. He has a small force only – the casualties were heavy. We expect attack. We may be outnumbered, *m'sieur*.'

'Come aboard,' Cameron said. Beside him, Petty Officer Osbaldston emanated suspicion: Frogs were Frogs and bloody liars with it. Back in the peace, a French destroyer had come into Pompey on a goodwill visit. Osbaldston had been engaged to a girl who worked in Boots in Palmerston Road in Southsea, where the naval officers and other nobs lived. Then the Frog boat came in. The girl's name was Ethel

Jones, couldn't be more British, but she'd fallen for oily Frog charm. The Frog equivalent of a sub-lieutenant, who'd taken Ethel to the Queen's Hotel and all, coffee at Handley's in the morning, she having skived from Boots, tea dances at Kimbell's in Osborne Road. She'd been swept off her feet and was now moving towards matronhood somewhere in bloody France. Mme Blom or something as daft. Her mum and dad had had the same view of Frogs as Osbaldston himself, but none of it had cut any ice with Ethel. As the Frog came aboard, jumping nimbly over the corvette's bulk-warks, Osbaldston covered him with his revolver and was glad to see Cameron also was taking no chances. Shepherded by Cameron and Osbaldston, the Foreign Legion officer moved for the bridge ladder.

Forrest met him at the head of the ladder, glancing interro-gatively at Cameron. Cameron made his report. Forrest, echoing the buffer, asked, 'How do I know he's genuine, Number One? If I land men to guard the mole, I deplete the ship's company – and we're open to attack ourselves. Maybe by motor-launches.'

'The fort could be worth having on our side,' Cameron said.

'That's a truism, Number One, but it all depends on the truth of what's been said. Meanwhile, there are those orders – they have priority.' Forrest swung round on the buffer. 'The First Lieutenant's coming below with me. Mr Perry-Grant will be in charge. Bring your armed party up to the bridge, and keep an eye on this French officer, all right?'

'Aye, sir,' Osbaldston answered, jerking his revolver. His eyes would be very well skinned. The Captain went down the ladder, followed by Cameron. In his cabin Forrest brought out a bunch of keys secured around his waist on a lanyard. Unlocking his small safe, he brought out the sealed envelope.

'Well, here goes,' he said.

On the bridge Osbaldston was watching Perry-Grant as well

as the Frenchman. Perry-Grant, all smiles as oily as any Frog who went off with engaged girls from Boots, seemed to fancy his knowledge of French and the two were barneying away like old mates, with the Frog waving his arms like a windmill. Osbaldston didn't understand a word beyond *oui* and *non* and stood on guard looking baffled and murderous. Every now and then as the French officer gesticulated Osbaldston believed he caught a whiff of scent, or anyway strongly scented soap, which all went to show that what they said was right and all Frogs were ponces, Foreign Legion toughies or not. He wasn't too sure about Perry-Grant, come to think of it. People who spoke French that well were suspect. Osbaldston was glad when the skipper and Jimmy came back to the bridge. Forrest caught the conversation and said in some surprise, 'I didn't know you had fluent French, Grant.'

Perry-Grant smirked. 'Many of my talents are hidden ones, sir. And I've found out a few pertinent matters.'

'Well done. Let's have 'em.'

'Very good, sir. This officer, whom I believe to be genuinely for de Gaulle – '

'Why? On what grounds?'

'A deep feeling. Here.' Perry-Grant placed a hand, inaccurately as it happened, over his heart. 'It's similar to the acceptance of a brief, really. One has a feeling for the truth, the truth or otherwise of a client's story. I'm not alone amongst barristers in that, of course. What *Capitaine* de Beaufois has said, hangs together.'

'And his news?'

'*Walney* and *Hartland* were both sunk – *Hartland* has blown up. There were very few survivors. *Capitaine* de Beaufois is sorry and offers his condolences and his regrets for the Vichy Government's actions. Word filtering through from the beaches indicates the operation not going wholly to plan. Some of the landings were late in getting ashore, and the landing craft were heavily opposed in some sectors. Also there was an uncharted sandbank off Oran – that didn't help.'

'I see. Well – '

'And *Capitaine* de Beaufois says the fort's artillery observers report the Vichy shore batteries put out of action by the British cruisers lying off – apparently *Aurora* was joined by two more from the covering force. Also, there are no Vichy warships left in the port – '

'Which explains the calm. Anything else?'

Perry-Grant said, 'I spoke about our casualties. There's a doctor at Fort Mers-el-Kebir. *Capitaine* de Beaufois promises his help in return for ours. *Capitaine* – '

'For God's sake use English!' Forrest snapped suddenly. Behind him Petty Officer Osbaldston felt like applauding; Perry-Grant's sycophantic, delicately-uttered '*capitaine*' was making him want to throw up. Perry-Grant shrugged. *Captain* de Beaufois, he said with an insolent emphasis, would ask his Colonel to send the doctor along with a stretcher party the moment he was back inside the fort.

'And what does he want from us?' Forrest asked.

Perry-Grant said, 'A patrol. Men to guard the mole and watch for Vichy landings from seaward. Cameron's already told you that.'

Forrest chose to disregard the rudeness. He said, 'We can do that from here – so long as we remain alongside, that is. Tell him that, Grant.'

'I hear for myself, Captain,' the Frenchman said. 'I speak English enough to understand.'

Forrest looked him up and down. 'Right. I'm taking a chance on you, Captain de Beaufois. I – '

'Please. I am sorry to interrupt. To defend from here will not do. The mole is long, the night dark. It is necessary to have armed parties all along, to act with immediacy – '

'I have a searchlight. I can illuminate the mole.'

'Thus inviting attack upon your ship, Captain.'

'That's true.' Forrest breathed hard down his nose as he caught another smirk from Perry-Grant. He'd spoken off the cuff, basically unwilling to put his ship's company at risk on the mole in order to pull French chestnuts out of the fire. For one thing, the weather was changing; his seaman's instinct told him that a gale was in the offing and he'd seen moles like this one before now, seen them gale-lashed and almost submerged, and it had happened with astonishing speed. Even as the thought passed through his mind there came a sudden buffet, a wind squall accompanied by the first drops of rain. There was a strong element of risk most certainly; but Forrest was in something of a cleft stick. He had to consider his wounded; and it became plain that de Beaufois intended using them as a lever. No British patrol, no doctor. And, overridingly, there were those sealed orders, now opened and digested. They involved co-operation with the French, the Gaullists; the Cross of Lorraine was a demanding one. *Oleander* might not be long in the port.

Forrest conceded. 'Very well, then,' he said somewhat stiffly. 'I'll make ten men plus an officer and a signalman available to patrol the sea wall, and I'll stand by for your doctor, Captain de Beaufois. Don't let me down. You understand?'

'I understand,' de Beaufois said. 'The stretchers – '

'My wounded remain aboard.'

'But in the fort – '

'I have no more to say,' Forrest snapped. He turned away. Perry-Grant began an objection: the fort, he said, according to de Beaufois, had excellent medical facilities and a proper sickbay. The men would be better off. Forrest said evenly. 'Thank you for your advice, Grant. You will see shortly that it's superfluous – and impossible.' He nodded at the buffer. 'All right, Osbaldston, you can draw off the hounds now.'

'As you say, sir,' Osbaldston said with reluctance. As the Frog took his leave and went down the ladder Osbaldston followed, his revolver still in his hand. What he wouldn't like to do with it . . . but he'd rather have done it with the whole bloody length of a Lee Enfield rifle. As he went down, he was hailed by the First Lieutenant. Jimmy wanted all hands mustered for'ard once the Frog was clear of the ship.

A few minutes later Cameron reported the muster correct and Forrest spoke to them from the bridge. 'I've always tried to keep you in the picture,' he said 'I'll make it brief. I'm organizing an armed patrol along the mole, by French request – *Free* French request. It'll be withdrawn at sunrise or at any time before if the officer in charge considers the weather unsafe or so bad as to inhibit any chance of an enemy landing.' He paused. 'That's one thing. In the meantime, as a result of orders sealed until now, I'm expecting a French vice-admiral to come aboard us. He was to have joined *Halberdier*, it seems, and both *Halberdier* and *Forsythia* would have had similar orders for the immediate future. However, they've both gone, so we have to cope on our own. This vice-admiral has recently decided to throw in his lot with the Free French – openly, that is. He's always been a Gaullist but till now he's kept it under cover, being ostensibly loyal to the Vichy government. Because of his knowledge of the Vichy forces, he's said to be valuable to Operation Torch. So we go on a special mission, not as strong now as we should have been: to take the French officer to sea and land him farther along the coast to the west, where there'll be a drop of Free French paratroops. More than that, I don't know yet. I assume the vice-admiral will enlighten me when he boards.'

That was all Forrest had to say. When he had finished, there was a buzz of talk along the decks. The events since Dunkirk had made all hands highly suspicious of the French and there was little trust even for the Free variety. A lot had been heard about General Charles de Gaulle, who was as tough as Monty himself and a sight more stiff-necked, even arguing the toss with Churchill, so it was said. On more than one occasion Winston had suffered the sharp end of the Cross of Lorraine and didn't go much on it. A case of no love lost but the war had produced some strange bedfellows. Look at Hitler and Stalin! The general feeling was one of reluctance to get involved with a Frog vice-admiral who could change his coat at the drop of a hat and had, apparently, led a double life until now, pretending to be for Vichy. However, there was no option about it. Orders were orders.

As the hands dismissed, Forrest came down the ladder. He all but bumped into Ordinary Seaman Passfield. Passfield, standing back out of the way and at attention, began an apology.

'That's all right,' Forrest said with a friendly smile. 'You're Passfield, aren't you?'

'Yes, sir.'

'I'm grateful to you. You behaved well in a moment of crisis, not to say near panic, and you steered splendidly.'

'Thank you, sir.'

'Don't thank me. It was you who put us safely alongside, Passfield. A White Paper's been started for your commission – right? I think you'll make a very good officer.'

Forrest walked on. Passfield was flushed with pleasure. The skipper had done his ego a lot of good, had redressed the balance of his dilemma in the wheelhouse when the coxswain had bought it. Passfield had been convinced he wouldn't manage, that he would pile the ship up by mishearing an order or confusing port with starboard, or something equally abysmal. He'd been very badly shaken by the coxswain's sudden and bloody end, by the stench of cordite, by the wicked sound of tearing metal and the close thunder and crash of gunfire. He'd almost vomitted and his stomach had loosened. But he'd taken a grip when he knew he had to and it had turned out all right. Except for the coxswain and the other dead, of course ... Passfield had a thought that CPO Hampson's family might appreciate a letter from someone who'd been with him when he died, but a moment's reflection told him that he couldn't write with any honesty, so better not to write at all. There was nothing except utter horror to write about.

As the armed party dropped down to the mole, now wind-swept and with rain lashing and a mounting sea driving hard against the raised seaward side, Cameron watched from the bridge, which was still manned. The lookouts were watching for any sign of the expected vice-admiral. The engines were still on stand-by and the ship was ready for sea; ERA Lott was on watch on the starting platform, deputizing for his chief who was checking round, feeling bearings for heat, watching his stokers moving about with oil cans and grease. Lott was indulging the reflex action of anyone whose life lay in ships' engine-rooms: wiping his hands on a ball of colourful cotton-waste. But Lott's mind was not at that moment on hand-wiping or even on engine-rooms. He knew his job from A to Z and when the engines were at rest he could allow his mind to wander while still subconsciously watching all he needed to watch: dials, gauges, steam pressure and Stoker Second Class Gimble who was about as much use as a whore at a wedding. Gimble just hadn't any notion of things mechanical and how he'd ever been accepted for the engine-room branch remained a mystery. But the lad was pleasant and willing and didn't mind a bollocking; so pleasant and willing that in fact a bollocking was very hard to give convincingly. Lott tended to leave it to Leading Stoker Riley, who was an Irishman of colourful language and had eyes like needles, very sharp.

Lott's mind was on his pin-ups. The impact of the French projectiles hadn't lowered any knickers, hadn't bared any breasts ... Lott grinned to himself as he thought about the expression on the 'swain's face when he'd made that jocular remark to Mr Cameron. Talk about prudish; then he remembered the 'swain was dead. Poor old Hampson – and old was the right word: he'd been a Fleet Reservist, called back off pension, happy enough to come back but at the same time hankering after the pub he'd managed in Pompey. He'd often grown nostalgic in the mess, sitting so far as possible where he couldn't see Lott's semi-nudes. He hadn't been brought up in the age of Jane and *Lilliput*. Ancient, Hampson had been. Believe it or not, he'd been a Seaman Boy Second Class at the Taku Forts, chasing the Chinks up the Pei-Ho back in 1900, after being landed from the China

Squadron. Forty-two years ago! Lott's mind came back to the present as he saw Gimble lift his oil can.

He yelled out, '*Gimble!*'

Gimble turned, one big grin. 'Yes, PO?'

'You don't bloody put oil there, lad! Not unless you want to sod up the system. Jesus give me strength. Don't you know any bloody thing?'

'Sorry, PO.' Gimble looked abashed, as though he didn't know, now, where he *could* put oil safely. Life was one big confusion, but one day he would do things right. He had ambitions; he was going to use the Navy to learn and when the war was over he'd be in line for what he'd always dreamed of: stoker-in-charge of the boiler-room at Sutton Coldfield General Hospital. He'd been brought up in an orphange – Dr Barnado's – and his knowledge of the world was small. It had been a shattering disappointment when after enlisting he'd found the Navy was no longer coal fired. He moved now out of the ERA's line of sight; what the eye didn't see the heart didn't grieve over, in the often-used words of the matron at the orphange. As Gimble vanished Lott sighed in sheer frustration. Then the telephone from the bridge whined at him and he picked it up.

'Starting platform.'

'First Lieutenant here. The weather's worsening. Warn the Chief, the Captain may decide to haul off.'

'Aye, aye, sir.' Lott hung up and sent a hand to find Chief ERA Makins. On the bridge Cameron waited for Forrest to come up. The wind had increased very suddenly, right up to gale force eight on the Beaufort Scale. It whined and screamed around the upperworks, set the signal halyards flapping and slatting noisily against the mast. Water was coming over the mole, flung spray mostly, but now and then in a solid wall of water that dropped with a sound like thunder to swirl and pound along the lower portion of the mole, the walkway that lay in the lee of the high rampart against the sea, before dispersing over the side into the water. If the men of the patrol got caught up in that lot it wouldn't be funny . . .

Forrest reached the bridge, nodded at Cameron, looked west along the mole. It was still dark; he could see little beyond the flung spray. He said, 'They should be all right if they have the sense to keep close under the lee of the wall. I just hope Grant has that much sense.'

'Self-preservation should help, sir,' Cameron said with a grin.

'That, or Leading Seaman Newcombe.' Forrest turned and swept the harbour with his glasses. So far as he could see the water inshore of the mole's unreliable protection was seething with white horses, with the wave tops breaking off in spume. 'I'll bet that doctor won't venture along the mole in this and I don't blame him. And no sign of the French admiral yet, either.'

'No, sir.'

'He's going to get a wetting.'

'Better than a Vichy firing squad.'

'No doubt! Well, if it gets any worse, Number One, I'll have to take her out. The wires don't look too happy – I checked round before coming up. I see you've put out some extra head and stern wires.'

'Yes, sir.'

Forrest was about to say something further when, a little to the westward of the corvette, along the mole towards Fort Mers-el-Kebir, an exceptionally heavy wave crashed over from seaward. Water was flung along the mole, moving fast, deep and heavy with a force that would have lifted any man in its path and flung him away like a cork. Forrest could only hope the patrol was by this time much farther west. At the same time the pitch of the gale increased, shouting aloud like the anger of the gods. Forrest looked alarmed as the ship rose and fell, with her wires straining to their limit as she surged against the fenders. He said, 'That's it. I'm moving off the wall.'

'Out to sea, sir?'

'Not with our landing party still on the mole. I'll head

59

inwards towards the fort, maybe nose her in when we sight them and pick them up. Or send a boat away. But that's bloody chancy in this sea.' Forrest gave a sudden shiver; the temperature had dropped with the gale's onset and already he and Cameron were wet through. 'Pipe the hands to stations, Number One. To start with I'll want her singled-up to the backspring.'

Perry-Grant, officer in charge of the patrol, was numb with cold, wet and panic. He could give no orders; he couldn't think straight, didn't know what orders to give. Should he take the party back to the ship, or should he go on? He was there to report by Aldis if there was any enemy landing but the Aldis had succumbed to the sea. He was about half way along the mole and it was equally dangerous to east and west. Dangerous where they were, too. The water swirled and roared in his ears, swept along knee-deep at times to knock him off his feet. Leading Seaman Newcombe caught him as he staggered, lifted him bodily and set him on his feet in the lee of the breakwater above.

'This is where we stay a while,' Newcombe said, sounding savage. 'Sir.'

'D'you think that's best, Newcombe?'

'I bloody know it is. Course, it may not be enough.'

Perry-Grant shook, his teeth clattering together, an action he was powerless to control. Forrest had been wickedly stupid in sending them on to the mole with this sort of weather likely to blow up, he should have been seaman enough to see it coming. Perry-Grant said as much to Newcombe. Newcombe said briefly, 'Skipper's all right. He has his orders. And he's a seaman. Not like some.'

'There's no need to be rude.'

'If the cap fits,' Newcombe said, 'wear it.'

'Sir.'

'What?'

'Officers are addressed as sir.'

'Bollocks. *Officers* are, yes.'

60

'I'll have you court martialled.' Perry-Grant was almost in tears. Newcombe grinned in his face and reminded him of earlier events that night. Newcombe was plainly very far from scared. Perry-Grant comforted himself with the thought, or anyway the hope, that Newcombe knew they would be safe if they just stayed where they were. After that, he said no more. As clear as Newcombe's lack of fear was the fact that he was now in charge. Perry-Grant read that in the faces of the men huddled beside him. They wouldn't take any notice of the officer till they'd checked with Newcombe. Perry-Grant had read similar expressions before, in London. He'd done an advice in his early days as a junior and it had been obvious that the clients wanted everything he said confirmed by his principal before they would take any notice. He had been unable to understand why; most clients were fairly witless and wouldn't have known the difference between a barrister and a solicitor's clerk, but they would never accept him. Now, on that exposed mole, he wasn't surprised by the seamen's reactions because he knew he was useless in such a situation. He began to pray for salvation, asking God's help in a high voice.

Newcombe said, 'Shut it. Let's have a little example to the lads, shall we? Defeatist, that's all you are.'

'To ask God's help isn't – '

'I said, shut your gate. I got nothing against God. But what we want now isn't God, it's the skipper. And he's sending help in.'

'What do you mean?'

'What I say. The *Oleander*, she's sent a boat. With bloody heroes manning it, what with this sea and all.'

Perry-Grant said, 'I can't see it. Where?'

'There.' Newcombe pointed, and moved out a little way from their comparative shelter. He sent a shout ringing across the turbulent water of the harbour, a shout that went with the wind's direction. He got an answer he didn't expect: a stream of tracer. It missed, and Newcombe turned away and ran back towards the others. He said, 'Correction. I got a sight of the sods in the rifle flashes.'

'Vichy?'

'Not Vichy. Sir. Bloody Huns.'

6

The wires had been cast off and brought inboard, an able seaman risking his life to nip ashore and throw off the eyes from the bollards and then nip back again. Forrest, moving astern on his engines until the whole weight of the ship came on to the backspring and she pivoted, gave the order for the last wire to be cast off and then put his engines to half ahead. *Oleander* moved off the mole, heading inwards towards Fort Mers-el-Kebir. The waves continued pounding over the breakwater, surging out towards the corvette and pushing her bodily across the harbour; Forrest passed helm orders to counteract.

Moving on, with all the bridge personnel keeping their eyes skinned for the landing party, Cameron picked up a boat ahead, crossing their course from south to north. He reported to the Captain.

Forrest said, 'Could be that vice-admiral. He's chosen a bloody fine time . . . wait a moment, though. I'm getting senile, Number One – he'd be approaching from astern, round the seaward end of the mole. *Now* what's in the air?'

'Could be the weather, sir.'

Forrest considered. 'Changed his tack?'

'Yes. Slid out of Oran by the land route and is crossing the harbour. He'd scarcely have used the mole, not if he had any sense!'

'I wonder if – ' Forrest broke off, then swore. 'Tracer, Number one – did you see that? Firing at our patrol, like as not!'

'Better draw their fire, sir. Looks as though they haven't

seen us yet.'

'Yes. Put the searchlight on 'em.'

Cameron picked up a sound-powered telephone. From amidships the beam broke out in a wide swathe, swung, steadied. The boat came up sharply, being flung about like flotsam. In the beam the Nazi helmets could be seen clearly; so could a machine-gun mounted in the bows.

Forrest said crisply, 'Man the close-range weapons, Number One. All spare hands to get for'ard with rifles. Engines to full ahead. Steer for the boat.'

'We're all right now,' Perry-Grant said.

'No thanks to you. Skipper's done it – the searchlight. Buggers'll be shitting themselves.' Newcombe was shouting but was only just heard above the wind's racket. There was still tracer flying around, but not in their direction. It was arcing towards the oncoming corvette, which was plunging about almost as badly as the small German boat itself. Result, the fall of shot was poor. Newcombe shouted again. 'Right, stand by to show, let the skipper see us. But watch it. I'll count the seconds between the bloody waves, then give the word.'

Perry-Grant's teeth still chattered. He said, 'What's the point of counting? The waves don't know.'

'Waves,' Newcombe said forebearingly, 'has a bleeding *pattern*. Near enough, anyway.' He began his count. As he counted, the corvette plunged on. Now the tracer from the Nazis seemed to be hitting home, smacking into the hull and superstructure. Then the close-range weapons opened up from the *Oleander*, the Oerlikons ripping their lead towards the German boat. Perry-Grant saw hands flung up, bodies falling overboard. The fire from the German fell away, to be resumed a half-minute later as another gunner took over from a dead man. *Oleander* was rushing on under full power, straight into the tracer. Then she hit. The boat, taken right amidships, disintegrated into matchwood, her after part floating fragmented down the corvette's starboard plating.

Heads were seen briefly in the water, lit by the searchlight as it swept astern. They were not seen for long.

'*Right!*' Leading Seaman Newcombe shouted. Perry-Grant felt himself propelled onwards by a hefty shove in the back. All the seamen moved out towards the lip of the mole and, to Newcombe's order, began yelling and waving their arms. Newcombe said, 'Once the skipper's seen us, stand by to run back for shelter – I'll give the word.'

A moment later they were picked up by the searchlight.

'There's too much weight of water to put her alongside for long enough if at all,' Forrest said, strain showing in his face and voice. By now there was a watery dawn breaking through, and the mountainous country on three sides was beginning to come up, stark and grey. The seas were almost level with the top of the breakwater, built up massively by the weight of the roaring, tempestuous wind. It was as though the whole Mediterranean was poised to pour over the top.

'I can take a boat away, sir. Volunteer crew.'

'Sheer suicide, Number One. God, I should never have put men out there on the say-so of that Foreign Legion fellow!'

'Exigencies of the service, sir, that's what they say. You had no option.'

'We won't argue about it, Number One.' Forrest was raking the mole with his binoculars; the men had vanished again, withdrawn into their more-or-less safe lee, but they couldn't last for long, certainly not until the weather moderated. The water's action would suck them out before long, swill them away into the harbour to be tossed eventually on to the shore, corpses all. 'It's the devil,' Forrest said almost in anguish – blaming himself again. He had another worry, too: that French vice-admiral. He still hadn't shown, and if he did, it was going to be touch-and-go whether he could be embarked.

Forrest said, 'Bugger TSGO.'

65

'Why, in particular, sir?'

'They don't embrace French admirals in boats in filthy weather. In other words, decision's called for on that score. But it can wait. There's only one thing for it as regards those poor devils on the mole: they'll have to jump for it between waves, and I'll stand in as close as I can. Get the scrambling nets out, Number One, and take charge for'ard. Kollenborne to go aft. Tell the buffer.'

'Aye, aye, sir.'

As Cameron went to pass the orders Forrest called to him. 'Just a moment. That idea of yours – a boat. It *could* provide a kind of longstop but it'll have to be done carefully, without undue risks taken. Willing to chance it?'

Cameron nodded. 'Of course, sir. The buffer can take over for'ard. I'll call away the seaboat's crew and lowerers.'

'Thank you, Number One. Strict orders: you're on no account to go in too close. The judgment as to how close is too close is up to you. But I'll not thank you for losing any more men. Or yourself,' he added.

Cameron went to the voice-pipe and passed the orders for the seaboat to the quartermaster, sending word at the same time for Midshipman Kollenborne and Petty Officer Osbaldston. As he made his way to the seaboat's falls he saw Kollenborne going aft, and called him.

'All right, Mid?'

'Yes, sir.'

'I'm taking the seaboat away. With Lightwell gone and Perry-Grant ashore, that leaves you and the Captain, just for a while. Bear it in mind. A lot's going to depend on you.'

'I'll be all right,' Kollenborne said. He sounded a little stiff: the inference was, I'm RN after all. Cameron understood, felt that perhaps his stricture had been unnecessary. The regular officers had a hard, exacting training from the word go; as cadets at Dartmouth they had been put through the mill by their divisional lieutenants and their petty officer instructors, trained from the start for eventual command.

On the bridge Forrest was thinking about the wounded

men below. By now there was no doubt left that the doctor from Fort Mers-el-Kebir wouldn't come along the mole. The chart showed a jetty running along below the old walls of the fort, connecting with the mole's western extremity. He might be able to find calmer water there, and nudge alongside for just long enough to embark the doctor.

'They're sending a boat away,' Leading Seaman Newcombe said. Then he saw a shaded lamp flashing from *Oleander's* bridge. The signalman was currently huddled with his shattered Aldis against the sea wall behind. Newcombe turned and prodded at a heap of misery. 'Right, Lofty. Signal. Read it off, right?'

Ordinary Signalman Cribbage did so. The signal was brief. 'Jump when ready,' Cribbage reported.

'Jump, eh. All right for salmon. Or bloody kangaroos.' Newcombe turned to Perry-Grant. He said sourly. 'We're about to jump in the hogwash and be picked up.'

'I heard what Cribbage said, thank you.'

'Just thought I'd let the officer know,' Newcombe said witheringly. 'And *I'll* give the word when.'

Perry-Grant said nothing; he didn't feel capable of making any contribution now. Everything about him felt slack, his limbs like jelly, his thoughts confused. The cold and wet had got right into him and fear had taken over his mind. He was convinced they were all going to drown now and then nothing would matter any more, even the fact that he now discovered he'd lost his service revolver. He'd groped for it with half a mind to threaten Newcombe with it; Newcombe's behaviour was bringing tears to his eyes. But it wasn't there; the flap of the holster was open. It had dropped out somewhere along the line and had probably been swept into the harbour. Perry-Grant shook; he covered his face with his hands. He didn't watch the approach of the seaboat in the grey dawn's dimness, didn't see the way it was bucking about, lifting and falling to the weight of green sea still crashing over the breakwater, didn't see the oars heave and miss the sea on the rise, and send the boat's crew sliding heavily against the stretchers, their bottoms thrown clear of the thwarts and their backs all but breaking against the wood.

Then he heard Newcombe's shout and felt himself shoved forward like before. 'Jump for it!' Newcombe shouted. '*Now!*' They all went forward, white-faced, grim, scared. Perry-Grant uncovered his face as he was propelled, willy-nilly. No one had bothered to ask if he could swim; as it happened, he wasn't a bad swimmer but this was no summer beach in England. He would rather have taken his chance on the mole, waiting for the weather to moderate even though at the moment it seemed to be worsening fast.

He looked at the boat, his eyes wide with terror. It was a long way off: fifty yards, perhaps, a long swim. The corvette, with her searchlight playing on the seaboat, was even further out.

All the others were in the water now, just bobbing heads surging this way and that, all except himself and Newcombe. Newcombe was staying to the last, really acting the officer. Then Perry-Grant was in, lifted bodily and thrown by the leading seaman into the boiling surge. Newcombe was beside him, urging him on. It was as though the man wanted him to live to suffer, just so he could go on tormenting him. Death seemed very close; but to his own surprise he found an instinct to live coming through and he battled on, with assistance. It was a gruelling business: there was a strong back-surge, and now and again the men were taken by this and swept as by a giant's grip away from the seaboat and back towards the cruel stone of the mole. Perry-Grant swam on, sobbing and screaming when his head was clear of the water. After a while he found he was alone; Newcombe had left him to it after all. He made progress nevertheless and began to close the seaboat, which was itself now moving in towards the bobbing heads and thrashing arms and legs. Perry-Grant at last found himself gripped and lifted against the gunwale, and then dragged aboard to collapse in a sodden, miserable heap on the bottom-boards, head down, legs trailing across a thwart. One by one more men joined him. Three did not; one of these was Leading Seaman Newcombe. He heard Cameron's voice, making the count and checking names. Perry-Grant was conscious of an immense relief. He lifted his head and stared around. He saw the mole where probably Newcombe had come to grief, swept back to be smashed by the surging sea against the stonework. Well, he'd asked for it; insubordination never got anyone anywhere.

Again he heard Cameron's voice, addressing him now: 'Three men unaccounted for, Perry-Grant. I can't hang around – there's the survivors to think about and we're making too much water. With luck, they'll make the scrambling nets.'

'Yes,' Perry-Grant managed to say. 'You're right.' Then he saw a hand come over the gunwale and heave a face level with the top strake. The face was Newcombe's and it was grinning like a devil, straight at him.

Newcombe said, 'Arse-end Charlie, that's me.' As his hand began slipping, he was grabbed and brought inboard. He looked at his last gasp and there was blood mingling with seawater on his forehead. The other two missing seamen didn't make it.

The seaboat hoisted, Forrest made his decision, for the sake of the wounded, to take his ship in to embark the French doctor. The increasing light showed the harbour strangely empty of warships. All seemed peace, though there was still the sound of gunfire to east and west where, presumably, the beachheads were not yet fully established. 'If at all,' he said to Cameron. 'I fear that cock-up, Number One.'

'We just have to wait for news, sir. Are you going to signal the fort?'

'Only if necessary. They'll see us coming unless they're blind. They'll know what we've come for.'

Cameron nodded. 'No French admiral yet?'

'No.' Forrest lowered his voice. 'I'll want a report on the landing party. Perry-Grant – you know what I mean?'

'Yes. There's what you might call an atmosphere, isn't there, sir?'

'You could cut it with a knife! I could sense it even from up here. I suppose that's what a captain's for. Well? A brief summary, Number One, as few words as possible.'

Cameron considered for a moment then said, 'Largely hearsay, sir, but I believe Perry-Grant's going to make a complaint about Newcombe.'

'That says it all,' Forrest said savagely. Cameron made no response. Within the next couple of minutes, with Fort Mers-el-Kebir not far ahead now, three Foreign Legion officers were seen coming down towards the jetty. 'No need for a signal,' Forrest said. Cameron went down to the upper deck to supervise the embarkation of the doctor. One of the Frenchmen was carrying a black bag; uniformed like the others, he was clearly a medical officer of the French Army. As Forrest brought the ship in carefully, one of the officers called up to the bridge.

'I am Colonel Chaumet of the Foreign Legion, now commanding Fort Mers-el-Kebir for General de Gaulle. I thank you for your help.'

'Thank the sea,' Forrest called back. 'The sea did it for us in the end. No attack could have been mounted in those conditions.'

'Yet you co-operated, Captain.' The English was flawless; Forrest grimaced at the words. He'd co-operated, and lost two men. He wasn't doing too well. 'Now I send my doctor for your wounded sailors. What do you propose to do?'

'Lie off while this weather lasts, Colonel. I have certain orders, and will remain in the port until they can be executed, although there's been a delay, it seems.' Forrest paused. 'Why are there no Vichy warships here – do you know?'

'All available ships are off the beachheads to repel your invasion.'

70

Forrest had more or less guessed that but was still surprised; the port had been left wide open once *Oleander* had got through. Maybe one little corvette wasn't worth bothering about and could be hemmed in and sunk just as soon as the Vichy mob were ready – there was just the one way out to sea, past the end of the mole. It certainly had all the appearance of a trap, but that had to be risked. His orders stood. As the ship moved alongside with fenders out, and touched the jetty, the doctor scrambled aboard and was helped over the bulwarks by a party of seamen. At once Forrest moved away, waving a hand and calling his thanks to the French Colonel; and the doctor was taken below to the cabins and wardroom, cleared for the use of the wounded men. When the ship was off the jetty, Forrest handed over to Cameron and went below to the seamen's messdeck, removing his cap as he stepped over the coaming: his steel helmet always vanished from his head the soonest possible. He found Newcombe bedded down on a hammock mattress laid along some locker-tops.

'Don't get up,' he said as the leading seaman lifted himself on an elbow. 'No ceremony, please. I've come only to thank you for – taking charge so well with Mr Perry-Grant. You averted a much worse tragedy.'

'Nothing to it, sir.'

Forrest grinned. 'Well, *I* don't underestimate it, anyway. Well done. That's all I wanted to say.'

'Thank you, sir. Did me best, that's all, sir. So did they all. We've a good ship's company, sir, barring some. That's down to you, sir, if I may make so bold as to say so. Some skippers is bloody awful.'

Forrest said gravely, 'I take that as the best compliment I've ever had, Newcombe.'

He turned away and started back for the bridge. Then, thoughtfully, he made instead for the wardroom where Perry-Grant would no doubt be taking it easy and recovering along with the wounded men, his cabin having been taken over with the others. But Perry-Grant forestalled him outside the wardroom. He looked half dead, Forrest thought, but something was driving him on and he was sure it wasn't duty. Sharply Forrest said, 'Well?'

'I was on my way to the bridge,' Perry-Grant said, his face awry. 'I've a serious complaint to make, I'm sorry to have to say. I believe it calls for a court martial – '

'A complaint as to what, or whom?'

'Leading Seaman Newcombe.'

'I wouldn't if I were you, Perry-Grant.' Forrest's voice was pure ice.

'But look here, sir – '

'Or do you relish dirty washing? *Do you*, Perry-Grant? I don't know all that went on along the mole, but I've got there to some extent and I'm blaming myself for having sent you in charge. But if you raise a stink, it's you the odour will suffocate. Since you're a lawyer, you astonish me by not realizing that without being told. I advise you to forget it.'

Forrest turned away, jaw thrust out, big body shaking with anger. Perry-Grant's near-hysterical voice followed him along the deck: 'Don't you know the first damn thing about maintaining discipline?'

7

As the Captain made his way for'ard the alarm rattlers sounded, urgent and strident throughout the ship. Forrest went the rest of the way at the double. On the bridge Cameron said, 'I'd just sent a messenger for you, sir. There's an ML entering.'

'So I see.' Forrest focussed his binoculars on the approaching motor-launch. 'Vichy flag.'

'Yes, sir, so I thought – '

'Action stations – quite right. But it's probably our French guest, Number One.'

'Under the Vichy flag?'

'Oh, a little more subterfuge till he's really got away with it. They don't look hostile. No guns manned.' Forrest continued looking through his binoculars as the motor-launch came on; she was clearly making towards them, and making very heavy weather of the confused, breaking sea. Seamen with white caps and red pom-poms, chin-stays down, could be seen standing by along the side. 'It's him,' Forrest said. 'In the wheelhouse – officer's cap at all events. The rest's covered with an oilskin. Stand by to bring him aboard, Number One – but only after he's given the code word.'

'Code word, sir? TSGO?'

Forrest laughed. 'No. Only now can I reveal ... there's a code word, specially for us and what you might call our sub-operation. On our part it's this: England expects.'

'That's all?'

'Yes.'

'Nelson lives again. And the answer, sir?'

'*Napoleon est mort.*'

'Someone at the Admiralty,' Cameron said, 'is highly original.'

It wasn't easy to get the Vice-Admiral aboard; the motor-launch rose and fell alarmingly, but, though big like Forrest, the French officer was nimble enough and Forrest saw him make it safely. Cameron escorted him to the bridge. The Captain saluted and his salute was returned punctiliously. 'Vice-Admiral Boulin?' Forrest asked.

'That is right, yes. *Vive la France, vive General de Gaulle.*'

Breezily Forrest said, 'Yes, indeed, sir,' repressing an impish desire to respond with Long Live England, Long Live the King. He went on, 'I understand I'm to land you handy for Beni Saf, south-west of Cape Fegalo?'

'Yes, that is so, Captain. For my part, I understood three ships – but am aware that two have been sunk. I am sorry. One ship alone, it is little enough, but it is necessary that we go on.' Boulin gave a deep shrug. 'There is no further availability. We must manage, you and I.'

Forrest smiled. 'Whatever it is we have to do, we'll do our best at all events. What about the paratroops?'

'They are to be dropped by Free French aircraft fighting with General Montgomery's forces. They are Gaullist soldiers of the Corps d'Afrique of France.' Boulin paused. 'You will be required to embark them – '

'*I'm* to embark them?' Forrest stared. 'I must remind you, we have just the one ship now. Where in God's name am I to put them? How many are there?'

The Frenchman said, 'There will be two hundred soldiers, but they will not be aboard your ship for long. They will not ask for the comfort of a luxury hotel!'

Forrest grunted. He asked, 'What about the ML, sir?'

'She will accompany us until we are outside the harbour. Then she will return to Algiers to join the fleet of your Admiral Cunningham. She came from there, as I myself did – I was not after all in Oran.'

Forrest turned away. There were things yet to be explained but they would have to wait. The first consideration was to get out of Mers-el-Kebir in safety, and the time might well be short: the entry of the apparent Vichy ML must surely have been observed from Oran or by Vichy spotters in Mers-el-Kebir itself; likewise the transfer of a man. Curiosity, to say the least, would have been aroused ashore. Curiosity was strong in Forrest's mind too: curiosity as to just what Boulin's mission might be.

With *Oleander* still at action stations, Forrest passed the orders to move out. Then he remembered the French doctor attending to the casualties. He said, 'You'd better tell that medic what's going on, Number One. Offer my apologies. I'll land him just as soon as it's possible.'

Cameron went aft. *Oleander* proceeded towards the exit, coming up to full power. There was no opposition; on the bridge, Boulin said he hadn't expected any. Oran's defenders were too heavily engaged to east and west, and soon the invasion tanks would be rumbling ashore from the landing craft on the beaches below the city itself. As *Oleander* reached the open sea the coastal batteries opened; far offshore the 16-inch turrets of the *Rodney* started a thunderous bombardment in reply.

Forrest looked at the chart. Not far to go: Cape Fegalo lay a little under fifty miles to the west, their destination of Beni Saf thirty miles beyond again. Boulin remained on the bridge with the Captain. As they left Mers-el-Kebir behind and the motor-launch detached, he made the suggestion that a conference of officers should be called. He would address it himself, he said, with Forrest's permission.

Vice-Admiral Boulin, it seemed, travelled light. All he had with him was an attaché case and some rolled-up maps and charts. These he spread out on the chart table. Perry-Grant, in his capacity as navigating officer, attended with Forrest and Cameron, leaving Kollenborne in charge of the watch. Also present was the Chief Engine-room Artificer, who had left ERA Lott to take over the starting-platform below.

Boulin was brief. He had, he said, special knowledge of the forces in the area, the Vichy and German forces, and their dispositions at the time of the main attacks; he was well able to make a good assessment of their subsequent deployment as those attacks developed.

'I have also other knowledge,' he said. 'Matters that were not known to the British and American commands until after the convoys and warships had begun their movements towards Torch. It is one of these matters that is the reason for my being here, and for your own movements immediately ahead.' He jabbed a finger on one of his charts. 'Here is Beni Saf. In Beni Saf is an underground stowage developed by engineers of the German Afrika Corps with the assistance of technicians provided by the Vichy government from the naval dockyards of Brest and Toulon and Marseilles. This has never been known to the British, for to all intents and purposes the harbour of Beni Saf is a mere anchorage for coastal craft – '

'Even from the air?' Forrest asked.

'Even from the air, yes. And as such not worth attacking, though in fact an occasional raid has been made, just, I think, to let the Nazis know that the British are alert and watchful. Nothing beyond that. The Germans have never been worried. But Beni Saf is more than a coastal port. In Beni Saf lies the Nazi ability to inhibit totally all the current operations. If the Germans so decide, Torch can be brought to a stop within a matter of hours. A total stop.'

Forrest frowned. It didn't seem to add up. 'If it's that big, why didn't the Allies react earlier? You've just said they got the information after the shipping movements had begun, and indeed the fact I was given my sealed orders in Gibraltar only two days ago supports that. But they've had time to change the orders. Surely an immediate attack could have been mounted?'

Boulin said, 'No, Captain. The information of what is *now* known to be in Beni Saf came to me only hours ago, by a coded radio message from a man inside Oran – a message that may or may not have been intercepted by Vichy. It is true that the Allies sent you, true that they wish the installation at Beni Saf to be destroyed. But, you see, they believe still – and I did until now – that the small coastal harbour of Beni Saf, so innocuous to see, is cover for a midget submarine base. Nothing more than that.'

Forrest snorted. 'Bad enough, surely?'

'But yes, to an extent. And certainly to be attacked. But not vital enough to put in jeopardy the secrecy of Operation Torch by mounting an attack as soon as the apparent facts were known. As I understand, it was decided at a high level that in the early stages of the invasion it would be better if the base were cut off only, which has indeed been done. British troops – if the westward sector landings have been successful – will now be in position between Beni Saf and the landing beaches.'

Forrest felt a degree of bewilderment still. He asked, 'Couldn't the place be attacked from the air?'

'Most positively not.' Boulin spread his hands wide. 'To do that would be in all ways quite fatal.'

'Why, for God's sake?'

'Because of the true nature of the base.' Boulin's face was hard, the mouth drawn down to form deep lines. 'To blow it up would be the end for most of North Africa, and would play into the Nazis' hands. With this is linked the reason why the Nazis have not yet used what is there to use. It is a last resort, and will be used when things move finally against them. Not before then. But *then* . . . yes, it will be used.'

Forrest caught Cameron's eye and gave a fractional wink. Boulin seemed to like the build-up of drama; his voice was solemn, portentous. There was something of the actor about him; Forrest brought him to the point.

'This thing they'll use,' he said. 'What is it, Admiral?'

'Anthrax,' Boulin said.

It had hit them like a bomb. Forrest, as *Oleander* headed up towards Cape Fegalo and distant British warships came into view, standing guard over the beachheads to their south, was still in a state of shock and disbelief that anything so appalling could even be considered by a government that, like Britain herself, called itself Christian. But Boulin had not minced his words. He reminded Forrest that Britain herself had carried out experiments on the remote Scottish island of Gruinard that had been impregnated with anthrax. As events had turned out Hitler had got the answers first, together with the wherewithal to apply them to combat. He wasn't the man to hold back if and when he saw defeat coming up; and Boulin had reason to know that the Nazi grip on North Africa was considered of vital importance in the German Chancellery, even to the extent, presumably, of saturating the earth of the coastal areas with the anthrax spores as a final and lasting form of revenge.

That was when Forrest had mentioned Montgomery and his Eighth Army, now fighting westwards from El Alamein. Yes, Boulin had said simply, they also would meet the contagion. Shaken rigid, Forrest had asked if Boulin had passed his new information to Admiral Cunningham. He had not; there had been only Vichy code books aboard the ML, codes that might not be in the possession of the Allied command, while any signal would be intercepted by the Vichy forces. For similar reasons he had vetoed Forrest's suggestion that the *Oleander*'s W/T be used: nothing, he said, was to be put at risk at this stage.

Recalling that conversation now, Forrest gripped the bridge rail, hard. He said, 'It's stunned me, Number One. It's incredible! I suppose Boulin knows what he's talking about. What did he say? Malignant tumours on contact with the skin. Humans and animals. It's murder of a whole country, its whole living population, everything that moves! Two million small bombs of it stockpiled in Beni Saf. *Two million.*'

Boulin had indicated the location. Two million canisters brought in by sea from Germany through French ports on the

Mediterranean, most of it very recently, possibly as a result of leaks about Operation Torch. Toulon, Marseilles ... they'd had no idea of what they'd been handling. Now it was all stored in deeply-dug, concrete-roofed pits behind the little, hitherto inoffensive township. Little more than a village really, and now it held North Africa and possibly more than North Africa in its hands. The reason for Boulin's insistence on a 'no-bombing' policy had become only too clear: even if bombs could have penetrated the concrete, they would only have scattered the anthrax spores and done the Nazis' work for them.

Boulin had not been specific as to how the threat might be nullified; it was, he said, a decision for the paratroops. They would know what to do. It should be straightforward: simply capture the base and hold it until the Allied armies moved in with the medical details who would be able to cope.

Forrest found his hands shaking; he tightened his grip instinctively on the guardrail: the Captain must not be seen to be in a state of nerves. And he must, as he always did, give his ship's company the facts. Meanwhile he wondered about Boulin's part in all this; why not leave it to the British and American invasion troops? Beni Saf wasn't all that far off the western end of the central assault area and could surely be dealt with as part of the whole. Forrest suspected French pride was behind it. Boulin's original mission had been to seize or blow up a midget submarine base, a foray that surely, whatever Boulin had said, could have been shoved into the overall operation even at such a late hour, but no; the French concept of military honour had intervened. De Gaulle had wished, perhaps, for Beni Saf to fall into Free French hands and had imposed his will on the War Cabinet and on the Pentagon, overriding TSGO ...

'I'll have a word with that doctor from the Fort,' Forrest said. 'I like to know precisely what I'm up against!'

Midshipman Kollenborne, with the rest of the officers, had listened to what the Captain had to say. Forrest had been very direct. He had explained what anthrax was: a loath-some disease transmitted through a skin abrasure, by swallowing, and by breathing. Under normal conditions it could come from wool, camel or goat's hair, hides and skins, bristles, horse-hair. The anthrax bacillus had been isolated in 1850 by a man called Devaine. The incubation period was a maximum of three days. If caught by breathing – the most likely in the present situation – internal anthrax would develop and the result would be swellings and ulcers and hae-morrhage in the intestines and the bronchioles, or lungs; and the bacteria could spread through the lymphatic circulation to cause secondary ulcers in any organ you cared to mention, plus typhoid symptoms. There was an anti-anthrax serum but needless to say none was available to the medics in North Africa – or at any rate far from enough to have any impact whatsoever after two million canisters had been dispersed. If the bacteria entered any abrasion, say from shaving, then death would come through syncope or oedema – fall in blood pressure or dropsy to the layman – and by the throat becoming affected by oedematous pustules. And death would come quickly. Not that alone: the land itself would die, for the infection would remain in the soil for decades. Maybe a hundred years or more, four generations.

'One way,' Forrest had ended, 'of ensuring that North Africa remains forever Nazi.'

Kollenborne shivered, feeling icy fingers pressing him into a North African grave. But the Captain had said nothing about landing parties. That was the paratroops' job; and Kollenborne wished them all the success in the world. Already he felt unclean, as though the off-shore wind – it had backed right round now – bringing with it the unmistakable smell of the African continent, was bringing also the disgust-ing spores.

He dreaded the next orders from the Captain. It was pretty clear that *Oleander* was detailed to take the paratroops, if not right into Beni Saf, then uncomfortably close. Kollenborne, trying to look as though he wasn't doing so, glanced at the reflection of his face in the glass of the signalling projector as he left the bridge on relief by Perry-Grant. He could have a pustule already. It wasn't just estate agents; he had a phobia about disease as well. The SP glass wasn't very revealing; he would have to find a mirror. He was on this errand when, through improving weather, a strong force of Fleet Air Arm fighter-bombers was seen coming in from the north where the aircraft carriers lay. They passed overhead and minutes later explosions were heard, faintly. That would be the Vichy airfield at La Senia coming under attack. It was the off-shore wind that brought the sounds; it could also bring churned-up dust. The anthrax spores probably hadn't been released yet, but Kollenborne hurried below.

On the bridge Cameron watched for the return of the aircraft. When they reappeared, they were all present and intact. Half an hour later *Oleander*'s course was crossed by a destroyer making in for the western beaches, and Forrest spoke to her captain through his loud hailer, asking for news. The landings were proceeding but were somewhat behind on their schedule; and Tafaroui, the main airfield, was still firmly in Vichy hands.

8

CONTACT was expected to be made with the Free French airborne troops at 1100 hours. They were to be dropped a little south of Cape Fegalo and as soon as they were seen to have landed *Oleander* would head in for the beach and lie off as close inshore as possible. Boats would be sent away to bring off the troops in relays. When the embarkation was complete *Oleander* would head back to lie off the western invasion beaches until dark, when she would move towards the coastal village of Ain-el-Basr, where the troops would be put ashore with Vice-Admiral Boulin. Boulin would guide them to the anthrax pits behind Beni Saf, and at a pre-arranged signal – three flashes from an Aldis on high ground – *Oleander* would move in to carry out a diversionary bombardment of the port; and Boulin would establish radio contact with Algiers once he had secured the pits.

Forrest, acutely aware that originally the plan had included *Halberdier* and *Forsythia*, didn't see a lot of hope. In an aside to Cameron he said, 'They'll be mown down in minutes. The Nazis'll be guarding that dump like a nun's virginity.'

'No other way, is there?'

Forrest shrugged. 'It seems not.' He'd asked Boulin why the paratroops couldn't be dropped directly on to the target; the Frenchman had been precise about that: they wouldn't have a chance. What hope there was lay in the clandestine approach from ground level. The airlift to the vicinity of Cape Fegalo was being made simply in the interest of getting them quickly into the area. Forrest went on, 'The nub of the whole damn show lies in the fact the pits can't be blown up!'

'I imagine anthrax is something you can't destroy easily in any case. How *do* you do it – burning, drowning, burying?'

Forrest shook his head doubtfully. 'Don't ask me. Burning's the most likely, I suppose. Anyway, that's not our worry.' He brought up his binoculars and studied the line of the shore as the corvette came round Cape Fegalo. Here there had been no landings; but back to the eastward the tanks were still moving ashore from the landing craft, pushing through the shallows and up the beaches into what sounded like a heavy curtain of fire. As Perry-Grant left the bridge with permission to visit the heads Forrest said restlessly, 'Our worries are ship-bound – right, Number One?'

Cameron sensed what was behind the remark: Perry-Grant and Leading Seaman Newcombe. He knew that Forrest had taken Perry-Grant's shouted remark more to heart than he need have done: *Don't you know anything about maintaining discipline?* Certainly, it was important to uphold an officer's authority, but, in Cameron's view, not when that officer had already made an abject exhibition of himself in front of ratings. Any upholding would have been somewhat too late and could only have lowered the standing of the upholder. Forrest, however, was seeing himself as the cause of it all in having entrusted the landing party to Perry-Grant. There was relevance in that, but on the other hand there had also been an inevitability: someone of rank had been required and Cameron was needed aboard as First Lieutenant; with Lightwell dead Kollenborne had been the only alternative but not only was he young in years but was young for his age as well, hadn't quite the normal tough assertiveness of a Midshipman RN. With all these aspects in mind, Cameron did his best to respond to Forrest – to his plea, in a sense.

He said, 'I'd forget it if I were you.'

'Perry-Grant won't.'

Cameron nodded. He said, 'I could have a word with him, sir. Off the record. Find out what happened, and point out the value of discretion . . . if the circumstances are what we seem to be suspecting.'

'Thank you, Number One. That might fill the bill. You won't get the truth, but you'll be able to read between the lines I imagine. I'm not keen to make it official.'

'Right, sir, consider it done. It's what a First Lieutenant's for.'

Forrest drummed his fingers on the bridge screen, his thoughts shifting. There was a fear in his mind that some dashing RAF type, believing Beni Saf to contain that midget submarine base and nothing else, might rush in with a bomb load even though the operation was being left to the Free French. As his worries nagged at him there was a report from the W/T office: a general signal from one of the offshore carriers that aircraft were approaching from the east. They were not indicating IFF; but the friend-or-foe indication wasn't always to be relied on even when it was present. Forrest bent to the voice-pipe.

'Stand by 4-inch and close-range weapons,' he said. Straightening, he spoke again to Boulin. 'Could be your paratroops, sir, they're about due. But we won't take any chances.'

He raked the eastern sky with his glasses, as did all the other bridge personnel. There was a small tic in Boulin's cheek as he waited for the oncoming aircraft to show. Throughout the ship men stood ready and expectant. Forrest looked round as Perry-Grant came back to the bridge. He said, 'Aircraft approaching from the east, Grant. Stand by to head inshore.'

'Aye, aye, sir.' Perry-Grant bent to the azimuth circle and took some bearings, checking the ship's position.

Stoker Second Class Gimble was currently out of sight from the starting platform, wielding his oil-can in more or less the right places. As ever in engine-rooms, there was a good deal of noise and as a result Gimble's toneless whistling remained unheard. Gimble was well aware that the Chief ERA didn't like whistling in his engine-room, neither did ERA Lott. The Chief had once told him, irately, that you never whistled purposelessly at sea: reason, traditional – like everything else in the Andrew. Likely enough Nelson hadn't whistled. Whether he had or not, it seemed that whistling brought on a wind and in the days of sail you hadn't whistled unless you'd wanted a gale. Sail was no more but you still didn't whistle. Gimble thought it daft but was willing enough to co-operate with Chiefy, who was a decent old stick most of the time; when Gimble did whistle, as now, it was totally unconscious, a sort of reflex action indicating various things: happiness, misery, being chokka, or just plain scared. Currently Gimble was scared. The Captain had spoken briefly, factually, and had intended to be reassuring, but that anthrax sounded vicious and they looked like going slap into it before long. The engine-room complement wouldn't be directly concerned, but the germs could penetrate presumably, coming in through the ventilators or somewhere, would probably even get through the air-lock that formed the seal that kept the pressure that stopped the boilers flashing back with fiery results ... Gimble oiled and whistled and scared himself more and more with his own thoughts. Bombs and guns and torpedoes, they were different. By comparison with disease germs they were clean. They were the sort of things you expected to tangle with when you joined up – and Gimble had joined as a volunteer, not as a conscript, being under the age for compulsory service. He'd had a vague idea what he was in for and it hadn't worried him. After all, torpedoings and that, they always happened to someone else, not to you. Gimble had been happily convinced that he would come through the war, right up until the time, that morning, when the skipper had talked about anthrax.

It was a real worry and all. ERA Lott hadn't helped much; when approached for advice and reassurance Lott had yelled back above the engine-room sounds that if he didn't watch his duties he'd get a bloody sight more than anthrax, to wit, a boot up the backside.

Gimble moved into the boiler-room, almost without realizing where he was going. He didn't see dials and gauges and hand-wheels; he saw millions and millions of bugs, advancing like the tide, bringing horror. He didn't know what the symptoms were; on joining he'd had, along with all the other new entries, a lecture on VD by a surgeon lieutenant, but anthrax hadn't been touched on. Stoker First Class Wright, a mate of Gimble's, had said it was much worse than VD, which was at least curable if you had the patience. Besides, Wright had said with a leer, VD was more fun to acquire. Wright had had several goes of clap himself and didn't seem all that worried about getting something else; he was the sort that took what came.

Gimble mooned about, looking as though he was busy. The stoker petty officer of the watch was in a huddle with a leading stoker and was taking no notice. Without any conscious thought, like his whistling, Gimble laid a hand on a large wheel of shining brass and at that moment the ship turned under full helm, heeling sharply and throwing Gimble off balance.

The aircraft had come in, four fat-bellied transports, and identification signals had been exchanged. Forrest let out pent-up breath and said, 'All's well, Number One. We head inshore as soon as the drop's been made,' he added to Perry-Grant. He lowered his binoculars, glancing at Boulin. The French Admiral still had his glasses up and a moment later he called to Forrest, his voice tense.

'There are more aircraft!'

'Fighter cover,' Forrest said, and once again brought his own glasses to bear.

'Fighters, yes. Cover, no. There are Nazi markings, Captain.'

'Jesus Christ, you're right! Tafaroui, probably. Nothing we can do, if I open with the heavy ack-ack I'll endanger the transports. Let's hope the carriers have spotted the bastards.'

They watched in growing apprehension as the fighters screamed in, weaving rings around the transports and spitting venom like airborne snakes. One of the big aircraft started to lose height, black smoke pouring from two of its engines, and a moment later men were seen to jump. As the parachutes opened, the Nazi fighters were in amongst them, spitting flame. Forrest and the others watched in terrible frustration as another of the transports went, bursting into a ball of fire. For a while the other two flew on, but the attack had been mounted in strength, some twenty fighters. The third lost height rapidly and turned over, then plummeted to the ground. A pall of smoke went up behind Cape Fegalo.

Savagely Forrest said, 'What a bloody balls-up! No fighter cover ... some staff bugger ought to be bloody well shot! And where are the bloody carriers, *our* carriers?' He stared into the sky helplessly. 'There goes the last one,' he said. The fourth transport, losing height like its companions, veered to starboard and made out over the sea, trailing smoke and followed by four of the fighters. It passed over the corvette and the watchers on the bridge saw the paratroops clustered ready to drop; but by now they hadn't the height.

Forrest said, 'Hard-a-starboard. Tell the Chief I want everything he's got. I'm going in to pick up survivors.'

That was when the corvette heeled; at the same time the fighters came in to attack her, swooping low above the bridge. The pom-pom and the 20mm close-range weapons stuttered out, but the Nazis came back in. A hail of bullets swept the decks, biting into the superstructure, both cannon and machine-gun fire. Flame appeared from somewhere and overhead the W/T aerials sagged drunkenly. Then, suddenly from the funnel, thick black smoke appeared, not a lot at first, but increasing. The bridge personnel coughed and choked as the heavy, greasy fumes swept back. Beneath it, the ship lay totally obscured as she headed for where the transport plane had now ditched. The attack on the *Oleander* was broken off abruptly; the fighters turned away, back for Tafaroui. Then Cameron saw British fighters coming in from the north: the aircraft carriers had reacted at last.

He said, 'They've just about saved us, sir.'

'Them and something else,' Forrest said. 'The Germans must have thought they'd hit something vital when they saw the Chief ERA making smoke – they believed the job done, I fancy!' He took up the sound-powered telephone to the engine-room. 'Chief? Captain here – '

The Chief ERA's voice came up full of apology. 'Won't happen again, sir – '

Forrest wasn't taking it in. He said, 'Quick thinking, Chief. You've done us a power of good – well done, even if it *was* without orders.'

Below on the starting platform the Chief ERA's face was a study. He said, 'It wasn't exactly me, sir,' but the Captain cut off in the middle. Chief ERA Makins wiped his face with his fistful of cotton-waste. 'That Gimble,' he said to ERA Lott, 'must have a perishing guardian angel, I reckon! Leans on the bloody hand-wheel and injects oil fuel when he didn't ought, sloppy sod, and skipper sends his congratulations . . . little so-and-so'll be rated up to leading stoker any minute, shouldn't wonder.'

There was more bad news. When *Oleander* had reached the ditched aircraft and brought off fifteen paratroops the leading telegraphist came to the bridge to report. Cannon shells had entered the transmitting and receiving room and caused an electrical fire. The damaged aerials could be coped with, but the transmitter had gone for a burton.

'We can still receive?' Forrest asked.

'At the moment, no, sir. But we'll cope. The transmitter's beyond repair, sir. Had it, sir.'

Forrest groaned. 'Do what you can, Sparks.'

'Yes, sir. But like I said . . . I don't hold out any hope.'

'Well, you know your job. I'll not demand the impossible. Off you go.'

The leading telegraphist saluted and went down the ladder at the rush. Forrest was feeling more and more frustration;

he turned to Boulin. 'That's virtually the end of your paratroops, I'm afraid, sir. Just fifteen.'

Boulin nodded. 'It will have to be enough,' he said.

Forrest stared. 'Fifteen men – to attack a place that's bound to be under very heavy guard? I wouldn't see much hope of success in that!'

'But with your men also, Captain.'

'They're not trained for land fighting, sir. Far from it.'

'You have a saying: needs must when the devil drives. The devil has driven hard, Captain. There is another saying in your Navy, that the sailor can turn his hand to anything.' Sweat had started out on Boulin's forehead and he spoke forcefully and with feeling. 'I ask you, I do not demand. I am in charge of the operation against Beni Saf but not of your ship. I ask you to understand the importance of dealing once and for all with Beni Saf and its filth. I ask you with all my heart to give me the assistance of your sailors.'

He said no more but looked beseeching. Forrest stared back into the French officer's face. It was a good face, the face of a man, the face of a seaman. The face of a man more than willing to risk his own life in what looked to Forrest to be a totally hopeless endeavour. Forrest said, 'Give me a moment,' and turned away to pace his bridge, deeply troubled. He looked along his decks, fore and aft. The *Oleander* was only a little ship, one of the Navy's maids-of-all-work, but he was proud of her, proud of her reputation painfully built up on the convoys out of Freetown, in the battles with the U-boats, in the unending work of shepherding the vital merchant ships. And he was proud of his ship's company, feeling protective towards them, unwilling to put them under French orders in an unfamiliar environment: seamen had never been soldiers, except briefly in the Naval Brigade in the South African War, again in the Naval Division dreamed up by Churchill in the 1914–18 lot. Well, of course, they'd done it then, and done it well. But they'd had training for it. That wasn't the case now.

Forrest met Cameron's eye. 'Well, Number One? What

do you think?'

'I think we have to give it a go, sir. There's something pretty frightful in Beni Saf. And we're the only ones now who can inhibit it. Or try to.'

Slowly Forrest nodded. Cameron said, 'I've had some experience of shoreside fighting, sir. Crete, and Norway.'

'Norway ... that DSC of yours. Yes.' Forrest went back across the bridge and met Boulin's eye. Boulin seemed to sense the answer.

'I thank you,' he said, 'from the bottom of my heart, and for France. *Vive de Gaulle. Vive La France.*'

Forrest wasn't quite so euphoric. He said, 'Don't get carried away just yet, Admiral. Before finally deciding, I'll want to know your plans in detail. I'm not throwing my men away on wild-goose chases.'

Gimble was relieved not to have been shoved in Jimmy's report but otherwise not too bothered. To him what he had done had been a normal enough reaction. If you were holding something and the ship lurched at that moment and threw you off your feet in a dangerous place like a boiler-room, well, you held on tight. If the thing you were holding happened to be the gadget that injected oil fuel into the furnaces and made smoke pour from the funnel – just too bad. He couldn't really be blamed; he didn't think much more about it, not even after the Chief had hauled him up and told him not to be so bloody stupid ever again, and never mind the fact that the skipper had acted ... well, Chiefy said with a curious expression on his face, not as he'd expected him to. It was high time, Chiefy had gone on, that Stoker Second Class Gimble tried to think himself into what he *was* in – i.e. a war situation. Gimble hadn't really thought very much about the war as such. But that afternoon he had to.

He found himself detailed for a stokers' landing party, to back up the deck ratings.

Admiral Boulin was keeping broadly to the *modus operandi*

already laid down for the seizure of the Nazi disease-pits: an approach by sea to Ain-el-Basr where the French force was to have been landed after full dark. From there to Beni Saf was a matter of five miles. The rescued airborne troops with *Oleander*'s seamen and stokers would cover that five miles as clandestinely as possible and attempt to surround the Nazi perimeter. After that, it was going to be a matter of bluff assisted by *Oleander*'s diversionary tactics.

Cameron was going in charge of the British party under the overall command of Admiral Boulin. With him he was taking Kollenborne, Petty Officer Osbaldston, and Leading Seaman Newcombe together with a signalman equipped with a battery-operated Aldis lamp. The rank-and-file of the naval landing party would consist of forty seamen and five stokers. With the paratroops that would make a total of sixty-six all ranks, French and British. Little enough, as Cameron admitted when he mustered the British detail separately and gave them their briefing.

'Just the same,' he said, 'we'll hold the line till the invasion forces link up. It can't be all that long.' He paused as he saw the sardonic look on Newcombe's face. 'Well, Newcombe? Got a comment?'

'Yes, sir. Is it true, sir, that one volunteer's worth ten pressed men, and a British serviceman's worth twenty of any other brand? I just wanted to know, like,' Newcombe added in an unctuous tone.

Cameron grinned. 'Probably. But you can do the multiplication for yourself – it comes to something like an army corps, I think. That's assuming we're all volunteers.'

They were not all volunteers, neither in the sense of not having been conscripted in the first place nor of sticking their necks out currently to catch anthrax. In spite of the Captain's factual exposition rumour about anthrax had gone through the ship like a dose of salts. Some of the imaginations were lurid: anthrax rotted everything, including the most vital part. It would drop off. Midshipman Kollenborne heard some of this and shuddered; in all truth there wasn't a lot of exaggeration. Gimble heard it too and, like Kollenborne, found all his fears of disease proliferating in his mind. His messmates, realizing the tizzy he was in, added their own fuel to the flames. Anthrax spores, they said, always first attacked those who worked under hot conditions, like you found in boiler-rooms. The enervating heat and the artificial light weakened the constitution and provided the breeding ground. Thereafter Gimble went around the ship as though every germ in North Africa was fornicating in his intestines.

So it had been a case of you and you and you, Osbaldston moving through the messdecks and about the guns with a stubbing finger and a voice that said there would be no argument. He knew none of them liked it; he didn't himself. But those filthy canisters didn't *have* to be broached; the Jerries wouldn't be any more anxious than themselves to be in the vicinity if that happened and presumably there would be a wholesale buggering off quick if there was an accident ... like, for instance, a stray bullet knocking a hole in one of the canisters. That wasn't likely to happen, though, not with the things down below in a pit. Osbaldston made much of this point: as he moved around on his distasteful task he said, 'Safe as bleeding houses it'll be. Them Jerries, they'll have 'em where they know they're secure, stands to reason.'

Talking to Leading Seaman Newcombe when all hands had been detailed he said, 'It'll be just like any other kind of attack. Kill Jerries, that's all. Don't worry what's in t'stores like, makes no difference, does that. There's another thing, too.'

'What?'

'The western beachheads. They should be secured by now, eh? There'll be troops not so far off.'

'Sure. Fully occupied.'

'Maybe not so occupied they'll not answer an SOS like. Anyway, just t'knowledge they're there should stop t'Nazis farting in church, I reckon.' Osbaldston went off, sucking his teeth and looking as gloomy as Old Nick. Never mind his attempt at optimism, he knew where he would rather be. Up in the North Riding, in the fresh cleanliness of the dales where the good wind blew free and the clouds scudded fast across the fells and the rivers clattered musically over their stones and waterfalls. Sod North Africa. Petty Officer Osbaldston went to the mess for his tot. The air attack had delayed the familiar pipe of Up Spirits but it took more than a bunch of Nazis to keep the Navy long from its rum. But he had scarcely lifted the glass to knock back his neaters in a cheerio to one of ERA Lott's nude women before the boatswain's mate was piping round the ship: 'All hands detailed for landing parties, muster aft.' Obeying the pipe, Osbaldston swore and went aft. The Frenchie was there with Cameron and some rolled-up bumph. Two paratroopers were detailed to tag on either side of a large drawing and hold it aloft for all to see. The Frenchie was quite a good hand at drawing, Osbaldston thought, and the anthrax pit area began to come alive, which was a funny word for anthrax. Boulin made it all look dead easy. In theory, the Jerries were dead already, enfiladed by a very nasty cross-fire.

Boulin ended by saying enthusiastically, 'After that, you understand, we go in, and – *whoomph*!' He threw his hands in the air. Osbaldston wasn't sure that *whoomph* was precisely the word to convey what the Frenchie probably meant; he certainly hoped it wasn't. Whoomph my arse, he thought, it had better not be.

9

'Stop engines.' Forrest's voice was quiet.
There was something about the night and its silence that
enforced low voices. The main fighting seemed to have
stopped; Forrest was avid for news but the damaged W/T
installation still wasn't giving any; they couldn't even get
the BBC's overseas news broadcasts, but at this stage the
BBC was unlikely to be precise in any case. Monty didn't
like his movements being made public before he was ready to
make his claims, even if he could be relied on to hog the
limelight when it was all over. Forrest found himself wondering how Wavell and Auchinleck would be feeling now.
Naturally, they would grudge Montgomery nothing of their
praise, but it had been they who had laid the groundwork
months before.

'Engines repeated stopped, sir.'

'Thank you, Grant. Check the heading.'

Perry-Grant looked down at the compass. 'One-seven-
nine.'

'Right.'

They drifted ghostlike towards the shore, damn lucky,
Forrest thought with a silent prayer for continuance, that
there was no moon. Long might that continue. He remained
on the port side of the bridge, watching the shore carefully.
Boulin was over to starboard, standing like a statue,
watching too, watching over the glory of France like as not.
There had been a few more *vive de Gaulles* flying around and
Forrest thought, cynically, that his ship's company could well
be back teeth awash with it. They wouldn't be fighting for de

94

Gaulle; they would be fighting, basically, for their families at home, be they parents, be they wives and children. Forrest wasn't entirely sure even that the King came into it all that much, popular though he undoubtedly was in the fleet. He was remote from their lives. But not so remote as the stiff-necked French patriot. For a moment Forrest's mind flew home across the seas and he thought of his former wife and the divorce. He wondered where she was now, what she was doing with her life. The man she'd married subsequently, her lover – was he in the Forces now? Either of them could be dead for all he knew. Forrest wondered what he was fighting for himself. Not Jane, not her new husband. There had been no children; and his parents had died some years ago. His brother had bought it outside Dunkirk, commanding a tank. His sister was in a convent, a closed order – when you were a convert you went the whole hog once religion had bitten. Like anthrax. Forrest was fighting for no one in particular. The King would have to suffice. There had to be something beyond oneself. There was always the country, but that would go to blazes after the war was won. The signs were there already. In the middle of a bloody great conflict, with all to lose to Hitler, the unions were busy impeding the work of the Liverpool docks among other national necessities. Behind Forrest a taut voice said suddenly, 'May I have a word, sir?'

Perry-Grant. Forrest said evenly, 'Is it important?' Something told him this wasn't about curent ship-handling or navigation.

'It is to me. I suppose it was you who sent Cameron to tick me off.'

'Leave it, Grant. Tomorrow's another day.'

'I won't leave it. I want an answer.' The voice began to shake. 'I want fair treatment.'

Forrest said, 'As Captain, I don't avoid my responsibilities. The answer's yes. And now leave it.'

'But I – '

'Leave it. That's an order. You'll disobey it at your peril, I promise you.' Steel had crept into the Captain's tone; Perry-Grant sulked but obeyed. His mind was in a turmoil. Cameron, senior to him certainly in his rank, was a much younger man, and unqualified where he, Perry-Grant, was a barrister-at-law. The whole juxtaposition was ridiculous. He was damned if he was going to sit down under it. His hands shook on the azimuth circle before him. Forrest was a boor, no education to speak of, seamen went early to their calling and after that they stopped learning. If he had to be in the Navy, Perry-Grant would prefer a staff job, one in London – the Admiralty, where his intellect could be employed. He was fed up with discomfort and the sort of people you found in corvettes.

'Engines to slow ahead,' Forrest said.

Perry-Grant passed the order down. Indecision, he thought surlily – Forrest had stopped engines too soon.

'Engines repeated slow ahead.' The ship moved on again, closing the shore – not far off now and nothing had started up, no guns had opened. Yet. But they couldn't be unseen for ever. Perry-Grant gnawed at his lip. He couldn't wait to get the landing party ashore and have the ship headed back out to sea again.

Forrest said sharply, looking over Perry-Grant's shoulder, 'Watch your heading. Come on, man! The course is still one-seven-nine.'

'I know.'

'Then get back on to it! You're five degrees to starboard.'

Perry-Grant said down the voice-pipe, surlily as before, 'Port ten.'

'Port ten, sir.' No coxswain now; a substitute PO. 'Ten of port wheel on, sir.'

'Midships . . . steady.'

'Steady, sir. Course one-seven-nine. Wheel's amidships, sir.'

It was all so repetitive, no wonder the mind wandered now and again. You didn't need any intelligence, just a sharp manner with ratings, a deferential one with your seniors.

That was the Navy. They went on; soon Forrest stopped engines again, and once more they drifted. Now they seemed to be enclosed by the shore, although they were well south of the headland of Cape Fegalo. It was an illusion really, existing just in Perry-Grant's mind because the corvette made him feel enclosed. The coast stretched flatly to east and west ahead; no lights were to be seen anywhere, it could be utterly deserted. Now Perry-Grant began to pick out the whiteness of sand, showing even through the night's blank darkness. Like a ribbon.

'Engines slow astern.'

More repetitiveness. The ship was brought up, the engines stopped again. Forrest said, 'In position, Admiral.'

Boulin turned. 'Thank you, Captain. We shall lose no time now.'

'Warn the First Lieutenant,' Forrest said. Perry-Grant sent the boatswain's mate away. Cameron was with the landing party, fallen in aft and along the waist on either side. He was joined by the Admiral.

'Now the camouflage,' Boulin said. Cameron nodded at a leading stoker, who came forward and daubed the Admiral's face and hands with a foul mixture of boot polish, grease and what looked and smelled like matter from the bilges. Cameron, irritated by the unnecessary delay, reflected on French fastidiousness: Boulin had refused to be daubed at the same time as the rest of the party. He hadn't wanted to be befouled before he had to, and, presumably, in this respect, sucks to General de Gaulle and France.

'Right,' Cameron said when Boulin's camouflage had been completed. He glanced round at his party: all hands were in seamen's blue jerseys and blue trousers, merging nicely with the night. Each man wore a steel helmet and carried a rifle, sheathed bayonets dangled from the webbing equipment. The paratroops were better armed: automatic rifles, Sten sub-machine-guns, M29 *Chatelleraux*, 2-inch mortars, grenades. They had a ferocious aspect and they were mostly lean and dark; the honour of France seemed visible in their determined faces. They would fight well, and to the death. 'All ready, sir.'

'Thank you, Lieutenant.' No more ceremony now; Boulin gave the word to go and the men slid over the side. The bottom was sandy, and Forrest had taken his ship in so close it was almost touching. Holding their weapons high above their heads, the heavier pieces being floated in aboard an inflatable rubber dinghy, the men swam, on their backs and using their legs only, until they found shallower water and were able to wade. They emerged on to the shore like shadows; Boulin had personally selected the spot for the landing. With his inside knowledge obtained whilst in the confidence of the Vichy forces, he knew where the land mines had been laid and where they had not. This sector was clear: they had a ridge of rock, narrow but safe, to thank for that. They moved swiftly up this ridge in single file, moving at its top into coarse grass with stunted trees beyond and sandy soil. Just a little cover.

Boulin halted them. He said, 'Now we move for some way to the south until we are clear of the coastal land mines.' Back aboard he had said that almost the whole of the coastal strip was heavily mined, but the ground to the south was safe. 'We remain together until I give the word, but now, so as to diverge more easily when the time comes, we split into the three parties as arranged.' He repeated this in French for the benefit of the paratroops, whom he himself would lead once they had closed the perimeter at Beni Saf. Cameron would take the second party with Leading Seaman Newcombe, while Killenborne, with Petty Officer Osbaldston, would command the third. The groups sorted themselves out quickly and then Boulin shook Cameron by the hand. He said solemnly, 'Success be with us, Lieutenant. *Vive de Gaulle.*'

From behind Cameron Newcombe said clearly, 'Oh, jolly good show,' in an exaggerated accent.

Cameron hissed, 'Pipe down, Newcombe. This isn't the time and place for you to be bloody unfunny.'

'Sorry I'm sure, sir.'

They moved out southwards, making inland, eyes flickering watchfully ahead and to either side, keeping in single file behind Boulin. It was an exposed feeling. The further they got from the ship the more exposed it became.

Kollenborne was finding that the rough wool of his seaman's jersey was making his daubed skin itch at wrists and neck. That made him think more acutely about disease. He scratched, and made matters worse. Nearly clear of the mined area now, they were moving through thicker-set trees, some sort of plantation – an orange grove, it could be, Kollenborne thought. The bark, which he impinged against from time to time, was covered in some sort of sticky substance and that, too, made him itch when bare flesh happened to touch it. He felt unclean but there was nothing to be done about it. Sweat broke out – and that added to his discomfort and his various itches. He didn't see this as a seaman's job at all.

The moon came up; Kollenborne cursed that gleaming silver ball, so pale and unkind. They would all be seen. Meanwhile they flitted through the trees with just a faint rattle of equipment from the seamen and stokers. Passfield happened to be on Kollenborne's left hand and the midshipman glanced at his face: the moon was bringing up the spots, great bluish-purple blobs. He looked ghastly, worsened by the cold light beyond his daytime appearance.

Back aboard the *Oleander*, Forrest was also cursing the untimely emergence of the moon. His part for the moment was simply to await the signal by Aldis from the landing party and his original intention had been to stand well off-shore and begin the movement towards Beni Saf so as to be ready when the signal came. The absence, until now, of the moon had led to his revised decision to remain a while longer in the vicinity of Ain-el-Basr on the off-chance that he might be of some assistance to Cameron if the latter should meet opposition behind the beaches. But now there was only one thing for it: he had to get out to sea before he was spotted in the moon-light. He said, 'Engines to full ahead, Grant. Wheel fifteen to starboard.'

Perry-Grant lost no time in passing the order down, wiping beads of sweat from his forehead. He began muttering to himself; and he failed to hear the next order.

Forrest repeated it. 'Ease to ten.' He paused, expectantly. 'Wake up, Grant!'

Something snapped. 'My name's Perry-Grant.' The voice was high.

Forrest shouldered the lieutenant from the binnacle and passed the orders down himself. He said, 'If you don't jump to it next time I give an order, I shall relieve you of watch-keeping duties. And after that I'll have you off the ship and under report.'

Perry-Grant was shaken by that. He knew what 'under report' meant: he would be reappointed for another captain to assess his fitness to continue holding a commission, a kind of second and last chance. If that report should be bad, then his commission would be terminated. It could happen; there was no need for formal and specific charges or for courts martial. He would be dropped from the Navy and would at once become liable for call-up as a private soldier with no hope of ever again being considered for a commission. And the war stretched ahead; there was no end in sight. North Africa was only one theatre.

'I'm sorry, sir,' he said grudgingly. The next order from the Captain was obeyed smartly. Below in the wheelhouse Petty Officer Bowling, acting coxswain, had heard the verbal exchange and was grinning to himself. Bowling was tickled pink to hear Perry-Grant get a bollocking. On the bridge Forrest wasn't so happy; he knew his voice would have trav-elled and he shouldn't have allowed his temper to get the better of him. He stared astern over the moonlit sea as the corvette headed north into the Mediterranean. All was quiet ashore. With luck everything would go right, but there was something disturbing in the very fact that the Germans hadn't reacted. It was scarcely conceivable that they wouldn't have mounted some kind of watch, unless of course they were keeping well clear of the whole area of the invasion beaches, falling back upon Beni Saf – and all ready now to start the drop of the anthrax canisters. Desperately Forrest wished for news of the Allied progress; the closer they came to victory, the closer came the ultimate Nazi threat.

Word was passed back along the line from Admiral Boulin: the advancing parties split in accordance with the previous orders, Boulin carrying on straight ahead while Cameron led his small force off to the left of the line of advance and Kollenborne veered right. By now they had the outskirts of Beni Saf in view, lit by the moon. They were still in the cover of the trees, and were on some gently rising ground with Beni Saf a little under a mile ahead. South and a little west of the small port there was another rise of the land; this rise was the leading mark. Behind it lay the target area, heavily disguised, heavily guarded: Boulin had spoken of a permanent garrison of 250 troops, mostly men of the Afrika Korps but including some Vichy details. Boulin had not been able to estimate how many more enemy forces might have fallen back on the port after the Torch beachheads had been established; all he could offer was the hope that there would be no more reinforcements now on the assumption that the Allied troops were advancing inland to the east of the port, thus cutting it off. The German garrison could be expected to have withdrawn in upon itself, self-contained and ready to go into action when the moment came. Boulin's tactics were simple: the hope was that, with the assault parties widely spread out around them, the Nazis would believe they were surrounded by a very much stronger force and could be duped into surrender.

It was a pretty thin hope . . .

It seemed to be a case of two minds with but a single thought: at Cameron's side Leading Seaman

Newcombe said in a whisper, 'I reckon we have to be bloody well barmy, sir.'

'It could come off.'

'*Could*,' Newcombe said gloomily.

'Don't drip.'

'Me, sir? I'm not dripping.' Newcombe sounded aggrieved. 'Just being realistic, that's all.'

They moved on. The absence of the enemy was almost uncanny; Cameron felt unseen eyes on the advance, felt that somewhere around them gunsights must be coming on. Prickles of apprehension attacked his spine. The atmosphere of a closing trap grew stronger. Half-way down the line of his party, Gimble started whistling. The sound ripped like a knife and Cameron swung round in a fury, but someone had acted fast. The whistling stopped.

It had scarcely done so when gunfire was heard ahead and the night was lit by flashes.

10

'THAT's gone and torn it,' Newcombe said as
Cameron ordered all hands down into cover. 'Looks like the
Frenchie's lot, sir.'

'Yes.' Cameron's instinct was to go forward to Boulin's
assitance but the French Admiral's orders had been clear:
each group was to act independently until they were all in
position around the pit perimeter. There was to be no assistance of one to another: the defenders wouldn't necessarily
know of the existence of the other parties and if attack
should come then those not involved were to carry on for the
target, taking advantage of the situation. 'Pass the word,
Newcombe. We go forward on our stomachs.'

'Right, sir.' Newcombe crawled back. The going was
rough as they moved on. Newcombe had a word with Stoker
Second Class Gimble.

'Bloody little twit.' Gimble's whistling obsession was well
known to all aboard the corvette. 'One more peep and I'll do
you.'

'Do you think it was that, killick?'

'What gave the game away? Shouldn't wonder.'

'I don't think it could have been. They haven't attacked
us.'

'Not yet, no. Now just shut up.' Newcombe crawled back
towards Cameron. The firing had intensified and the night
was loud with the stutter of the automatic weapons, coming
in sustained bursts. On their course to the left, Cameron's
group drew level. Stray bullets sang above their heads, a
powerful stimulus to keep down. As they crawled on,

making as much speed as possible, a figure was seen running hell for leather across from Boulin's group.

'Trying to make contact,' Newcombe said. The running man, one of the paratroops, had almost reached them when he threw up his arms and pitched forward on to his face. Cameron moved to the right, crawling towards the still figure.

The man, bleeding from a bullet hole in the back, wasn't going to last. But he was trying to say something. Cameron put an ear to the moving lips. The voice was very faint but he managed to catch the words. *'L'amiral...'*

'Yes? I'm listening. *Qu'est-ce que c'est?'*

'L'amiral est mort.'

The body gave a convulsive jerk and a sharp cry. Cameron felt for the heart: the man was dead. Cameron crawled back, told Newcombe what had happened.

'You're in charge now, sir,' Newcombe said. 'No officers with them paratroops, was there?' He paused. 'What's the orders now, sir?'

'We carry on,' Cameron said.

'Any point, sir?'

'Probably not. But we're stuck with it now. And there's still the old *Oleander* to back us. We've got to have a go.'

'We're the charlies again. Trust us! Roll on my bloody twelve. We haven't a cat in hell's chance and I reckon we all know it, but I s'pose you're right, sir.' Newcombe scratched at his face and neck. The crawl had given them all the itch by now. The firing ceased, as suddenly as it had begun. 'Press on, sir?'

'Not yet. We'll see what the next move is first.'

'The Jerries?'

'Yes.'

In dead silence, they waited. As they waited, clouds rolled across the moon. Dirty weather looked like coming back, but the absence of light was something of a bonus. Now the night was as dark as pitch. Through it within the next minute they heard snapped commands in a guttural voice, and then the

104

distant clank of metal. After that, silence. It was fairly obvious that all the Frenchmen had been killed or taken prisoner. Once again Newcombe asked if they were to move on. Cameron said, 'We'll give it an hour. We still have plenty of night ahead of us. Let the panic die down a little.'

'What about Mr Kollenborne, sir? Don't want him advancing on his own, do we?'

'That's a point.'

'Send a hand to make contact, sir?'

Cameron nodded. 'Yes. See to that, will you, Newcombe? Tell Mr Kollenborne he's to lie doggo till . . .' He pulled back his sleeve to look at the luminous dial of his wristwatch. '2300 hours. Then he's to advance in accordance with the original orders. But if Mr Kollenborne's party isn't contacted within fifteen minutes, the messenger's to return and rejoin.'

Leading Seaman Newcombe crawled back down the line. He found Passfield. 'You,' he said. 'In for a bleedin' commission, right?'

'Yes, killick – '

'Then you can show some initiative, lad. Officer-Like Qualities, they call it. OL bloody Q. Nip right and find Kollenborne.' Newcombe passed the orders. 'Manage without a nanny, can you? Officers usually has nannies.' Then he relented. 'Don't take too much notice of that. You'll be all right.'

Passfield was grateful for the confidence but he wasn't too sure. It was a dark night and he didn't know the terrain. Neither did he know with any precision where Kollenborne's group was to be found. But it wouldn't be the first time in war that a messenger had been despatched with insufficient guidance. Passfield took a deep breath and a grip on his nerves and started out.

Away to the right, with the third group, the one closest to the mined coastal strip, Petty Officer Osbaldston was to some extent acting as nanny to Midshipman Kollenborne who was

105

in a dither as to what he should be doing now.

Osbaldston said, 'Usual thing, sir, is to obey the last order. In which case, we carry on.'

'Yes, quite. But by now the Germans'll be fully alerted, won't they?'

'Don't make no difference to orders, sir. Admiral Boulin, he covered that. Take advantage was what he said. Go on under cover of any fighting.'

'But the fighting's stopped.'

Osbaldston thought: daft ha'porth, sure it has, and you've given us a nice long rest while you thought about it. He said, 'That's right, it has. Better push on now, sir.'

'The Captain didn't want undue risk to the men. I have to bear that in mind.' Kollenborne was sweating like a pig despite the night's cold. Every step took him closer to disease; he shied away from the thought that he was finding excuses. He didn't find it hard to see the continuance of the mission as sheer suicide and, as such, pointless, but deep down he knew the truth. It wasn't the pointlessness; England's history was glorious with the deeds of men who'd faced apparent pointlessness and come through to honour and a realization that it had been, in the end, far from pointless.

Osbaldston pressed. 'What we're going to do – it's vital. And I reckon we can still do it. The paratroops, they were just fifteen men. Doesn't make that much difference, now does it, sir?'

'It's not that. It's the alerting of the defence.'

'Sod that, sir,' Osbaldston said impatiently. 'We're t'Navy! Make enough song and dance and we'll have 'em eating out of our hand. Not that I'm anxious to cop a bullet, mind. But I wouldn't call myself a PO if I pulled back now, that I wouldn't.'

He'd gone as far as seemed wise. In the darkness, Kollenborne went a deep red. The inference had been all too clear and had struck home sharply. It stirred the basic training, the taut discipline of Dartmouth. You didn't shirk no matter

106

what. He said, 'We'll have to back up Mr Cameron, of course.'

'Of course, sir.'

'I intended to do that, naturally.'

'Yes, sir,' Osbaldston said, his tongue in his cheek. How the young bugger thought he could back up Mr Cameron by pulling back was a real poser, but never mind, he'd made his point. 'Move on, sir?'

Kollenborne said defiantly, 'Yes, PO. Pass the word back.'

'Aye, aye, sir.'

They moved on. They were back on their feet now and they moved fast. Passfield missed them, crossing ahead of their track, utterly lost now. He'd been given that fifteen minutes: he looked at his watch. It had stopped. Near to panic, he gave it a shake. No good. Was it fifteen minutes since he'd started out, or wasn't it? A would-be officer had to show initiative, but what the hell was initiative in this situation? If he returned too soon with a negative report, he certainly wouldn't have shown initiative and Cameron would bawl him out. That was no way to a good report, no way to a Captain's recommend for a commission.

Passfield's heart beat alarmingly and he felt stifled, all the signs of panic manifesting themselves. He went on through the pitch darkness, stumbling about like an idiot. After a while he caught the low glimmer of the sea through the trees. That was the last thing he saw. His foot came down on a land mine and he was virtually mincemeat from the chest down. When Kollenborne came up he recognized the face when he all but fell over the torso, blown some way inland by the explosion. Hastily, he shifted south; he must be too close to the minefield. Passfield, the estate agent ... Kollenborne, shaken by the sight of the remains, felt remorse for having snubbed him that day when he'd tried to open a conversation about Kollenborne and Pratt of Oxford. That had been an unworthy reaction, one he was ashamed of now.

Osbaldston, Passfield's sea-daddy, shook his head sadly. Too bad. The lad had shown promise. He would write a line to the parents, for what comfort it might bring.

Perry-Grant had reported gunfire from the shore. Forrest, who had already heard it for himself, swung his glasses but could pick up no flashes. They would be obscured, no doubt, by the trees behind the beach.

'I think it was rifle fire,' Perry-Grant said.

'And automatic stuff. Certainly nothing heavy.' Forrest swore. 'That's put the cat among the goldfish, by God it has!'

Perry-Grant said nothing. He had never imagined the expedition could have the remotest chance of success, believed Forrest should never have given his co-operation after the attack on the aircraft bringing the paratroops in. It wasn't the Navy's business; they had been made into nothing more than cat's-paws for Boulin. Perry-Grant didn't like his present situation; fear was loosening his stomach badly. The whole atmosphere was one of menace, of appalling danger to come. Forrest, as though talking to himself – in Perry-Grant's view the first sign of a creaking mind – said, 'I wonder. I've half a mind to go in right away.'

'Go in where?'

Forrest said irritably, 'Beni Saf.'

'That means action – '

'It does.'

'Don't forget we have wounded men aboard, and that French doctor.'

'I've not forgotten my wounded.' Probably Perry-Grant had until now.

Perry-Grant tried again. 'We're under orders, sir – Admiral Boulin's orders – to lie off until we get the word from Cameron.'

'I know the orders, Grant. But if the thing's going to abort, and it could if the landing party's engaged already, then I want to get them off. As many as possible, anyhow.'

'Surely they wouldn't head for the port, sir?' Perry-Grant's tone was long-suffering, as though speaking to an idiot. 'One has to look at this objectively. It would be too obvious – and in any case they wouldn't be expecting us yet, would they? I suggest they'd be more likely to go inland, or head east to make contact with the landing beaches.'

'You may be right,' Forrest said. He brought his glasses down and gave a heavy sigh. The whole business was very much on his conscience but if it could be brought off then his ship would have earned her keep all right. And you couldn't expect to bring anything off without casualties. He must not be too sensitive about casualties. In war you had to develop a tough hide. His part in Torch was small enough in terms of manpower involved; the army would be counting its casualties in thousands. But though the army liked to think of its regiments as families, there was nothing on this earth quite so close as the members of a small ship's company, especially in time of war. If necessary he would take his ship right in for the beach and hope that the minefield wouldn't pick off too many of his men before they could be got aboard.

'What are you going to do, sir?' Perry-Grant asked.

Forrest said, 'Await developments for a while.' Once again he made a binocular search of the shore, without result. 'I may yet decide to enter Beni Saf without waiting for that Aldis. It's obvious there's been a cock-up.'

'It's usually a mistake not to keep to orders, sir. I've read some naval and military history. There's general agreement that not to keep to the plan can interfere seriously with the intentions of the overall command.'

'Have you read about Nelson?' Forrest asked politely. That put the damper on Perry-Grant. Forrest had the strong impression that Perry-Grant had no wish to find himself any closer to the shore. He was thinking entirely of his own skin. Forrest found himself growing coldly furious with cowardice; one couldn't ignore the man, it wasn't in Forrest's nature to behave like that, but his very presence had become an irritation.

Just then there was a jag of flame from the shore, and soon after this the sharp crack reached them. Perry-Grant asked, 'Did you see that?'

'Yes. A land mine, I fancy. Just one.'

They waited, but there was nothing further.

'Thirty minutes,' Cameron said. 'No Passfield.'

'So what do we do, sir?'

'I'm going to assume he's made it and has remained with Mr Kollenborne's party.'

'I reckon not, sir. Passfield's the sort who sticks to the book. Tell him to come back, he'll come back.' Newcombe paused. 'That land mine we heard. Could have been him.'

Cameron said, 'Yes, I know. But it could have been any one of the other group. If so, Mr Kollenborne may have hung on to Passfield as a replacement. I'm sticking to my assumption. We move on, Newcombe, as soon as the hour's up. Thirty minutes to go.'

They waited, tensely silent for the most part. Gimble lay flat on the ground, consciously not whistling. His lips were virtually clamped shut and it was a big effort. Never in his life before had he wished so much to whistle and bring some sort of comfort. But he felt inside himself that his last whistle had been responsible for the heavy fire that had hit the Frog party. Daft, probably, but there it was. He'd whistled and the bloody guns had opened. Gimble was thinking back to Dr Barnado's. Years ago now ... they'd all been driven crackers by his whistling, or so Matron had said. He was always getting ticked off, stood in the corner when he'd been younger, given extra tasks to perform when he was older. One thing stuck in his mind: Matron had said, one day, that sooner or later his whistling would be the death of someone. Talk about prophecy!

He would never live this night down. They would all be blaming him afterwards, that de Gaulle and all most likely. Gimble eased his body on the prickly growth that sprouted up through the North African sand. He felt just as useless as the stoker PO always said he was. Useless and a misfit, the loony who made unauthorized smoke from the funnel and whistled men to death. He'd never been any good ever since he left Dr Barnado's and the chances were that, after tonight, the boiler-house at Sutton Coldfield General would be forever closed to him. You couldn't risk an outpouring of smoke in a hospital and you didn't want people who killed other people either. Not in a hospital. That stood to reason.

Gimble's lips started to open – that reflex action again. He flushed red in the darkness and closed them again. He didn't whistle but he sneezed, a very loud one, uncontrollable. An able seaman lying beside him lifted on to one elbow and said, 'For Christ's sake!'

'Sorry...'

'I could do with a bath but not one like that, dirty little sod. Noise, too. Wake the flippin' dead, let alone the Jerries.'

Gimble cringed. He couldn't do anything right. Close by him the AB, name of Gollett, a three-badgeman of sturdy stomach, gave a sudden belch, but quietly. He was conscious of the carrying effects of sound, always had been, especially at home, home being a tiny terraced house in Fratton in Pompey. The party walls were as thin as paper. Next to him on the left there had once dwelt a Leading Sick Berth Attendant from the barracks, a married man who was clearly over-sexed and could be heard banging away with his wife night after night, hour after hour. Felt, too. The wall shook. The sounds exacerbated AB Gollett till they nearly drove him mad with envy, since Daisy, his own wife, was disobliging three hundred and sixty four days of the year. Gollett had also been at RNB at that time and one morning he'd walked to the barracks with the LSBA and had been so far provoked the night before as to remonstrate. The LSBA, sensing the envy, had made a jeering remark about those that didn't get enough. Able Seaman Gollett, not diposed to take that sort of remark from a pisspot jerker, had lashed out. There had been a brawl, attended by the coppers, and they'd landed up in the police court at the Guildhall. Gollett had only been fined, since the magistrates had proved human and accepted a plea of provocation, but it rankled still. That was the sort of thing noise caused. Every time a gun went off aboard Gollett

111

thought about the LSBA. The reverberations of the recoil were just like Fratton.

At the head of the line, the hands of Cameron's watch showed the hour passed. Cameron nudged Leading Seaman Newcombe. 'Get 'em moving now.' There hadn't been a sound from the Germans.

Newcombe passed the word back. They crawled on over the rough ground with Gimble bringing up the rear. The moon was now totally obscured beneath a low cloud base; it was cold, and soon the rain started. It sheeted down, blown by a bluster of wind. All hands were quickly drenched through, pictures of misery dragging themselves over sodden ground. Able Seaman Gollett once again thought of home, or at any rate of Fratton Park when Pompey were playing at home and it was raining and the thudding studs churned up the ground and the weeping afternoon lay heavy over the sodden stands and terraces. Gollett had been in Pompey the year they won the Cup and extra leave had been given from the barracks to join in the cheering outside the Guildhall when the triumphant team had raised it high, but he hadn't made it on account of a sudden stroke of illness: he'd got pissed at lunchtime in the Golden Fleece and had passed out. He wouldn't at all mind being pissed again right now; he *would* be, when they came through this lot and maybe had a run ashore in Oran. French women ... the mere thought kept Gollett going. French knickers, lovely! Daisy wore blackouts, right down to the knee, some of them inherited from Gollett's mother-in-law and dating back to Queen Victoria. Not that it made much difference, except for the annual event.

Now leading Seaman Newcombe was on his feet and coming down the line with orders.

'Target's in sight,' he said briefly. 'Coming to the rise. We keep left, that's south. When we reach the perimeter, we spread out. No firing till you get the word.'

He went back to rejoin Cameron.

Half an hour later, moving on their feet now and moving

112

fast through rain and wind and dark lit periodically ahead by the glow of a searchlight, they were coming round the rise of the land. Cameron ordered them all back on their stomachs as they came into open ground westwards of the rise. A few minutes later he called a halt and studied the land to the north through his binoculars.

'That's it,' he said. 'Just as Admiral Boulin drew it. Take a look.' He handed the glasses to Newcombe. The Leading Seaman saw a kind of sheen in the ground slightly below their position.

'The concrete,' he said. 'Rain's making it shine up nicely and never mind the dark. Looks sort of impregnable, sir.'

'We're going to make it pregnable, Newcombe.'

'Any idea how, sir?'

Cameron grinned. 'Not a glimmer. I agree it looks what you might call difficult. We'll follow Boulin's notions – all we can do. Bluff and bullshit. It can work wonders.'

'Yes, sir.' Newcombe hesitated. 'No sign of Mr Kollenborne's party, sir.'

'There's time yet. In any case, they shouldn't show. If they're in position already, Mr Kollenborne'll wait for me to open first.' Once again Cameron looked through his binoculars, a long look. He said, 'Sentries.' Nazi soldiers were positioned right around the perimeter, meeting at intervals then turning about and marching back along their posts. This checked with Boulin's briefing, as did a tall watch-tower on the northern side, manned and equipped with sub-machine-guns and a searchlight, currently switched off. Cameron knew the entire perimeter was surrounded with a barbed-wire fence but this could not yet be seen. According to Boulin, the searchlight usually swept at five-minute intervals.

Newcombe said, 'It's a fair sod.'

It was; if the original force of paratroops had not been shot down the plan would have been credible enough. Boulin would have had an undoubted ability to leave enough weaponry behind to cover the perimeter while he advanced with his main body to establish a hold on the base. But it was useless to look over one's shoulder with vain wishes ...

'Go in now, sir?'

'Wait for the searchlight. I want to get the timing.'

The beam came on as Cameron spoke. He took the time by his watch. The swathe of light, blinding by contrast with the previous dark, swept to the perimeter and just a few feet beyond. It gave them their bearings; and the moment the light died Cameron passed the order to move. They were to halt when they were some thirty yards from the extreme sweep of the light or immediately when next the beam came on. When he gave the subsequent and final movement order they were to spread out, leaving as near as could be judged thirty yards between each man. Cameron would allow two further goes of the searchlight for all hands to reach their positions to right and left. The next time the light died, he would open fire. As he did so the signalman, who would by this time have detached back a little way to the rising ground in rear, would use his Aldis to send his three flashes, repeating until he was answered from the *Oleander* by a single flash and shifting his ground in the intervals to lessen the risk of being picked off by the Nazi defenders. When Cameron fired, all hands would follow suit, their point of aim being the sentries nearest them. Mr Kollenborne, Cameron said, would be dealing with the watch-tower. Or so he hoped.

Back on their stomachs, the men crawled ahead. The searchlight came on again. They pressed themselves to the wet ground and remained still as the light swept its ponderous way round. The concrete gleamed beneath the falling rain, a very secure roof for what lay beneath. When once more the beam died, Cameron gave the word to deploy.

The outward-spreading movement had just begun when sustained and heavy firing came from the vicinity of the watch-tower.

11

MIDSHIPMAN Kollenborne had advanced in a similar fashion to Cameron, ably supported by Petty Officer Osbaldston. Osbaldston was well used to difficult country and found no physical problems; he had an almost inherent sense of direction as well. But even he couldn't be expected to know something that Admiral Boulin had, it appeared, not known about either: trip wires laid across the distant approach to the watch-tower, which he and Kollenborne had had in view for the latter part of the crawl. Almost in the same moment as the men dragged into the wires, the sub-machine-guns started from the tower and the searchlight was beamed down full onto them.

'It's a bloody trap!' Osbaldston shouted. That was the last thing he said. Bullets tore into him, shredding him up and down, slicing him in half with a close line of holes. He sagged into a pool of blood. Immediately in front of him Kollenborne died with a bullet through his throat that before speeding on its way had torn out his voice-box. The seamen and stokers scattered, taken utterly unawares and anxious only to avoid the buzzing lead from the sub-machine-guns and the beam of light that was picking them out as targets. Not many made it. Of those who did, some blundered panic-stricken in the direction of the beach, right into the land mines.

On the far side of the perimeter, Cameron made an assessment. The searchlight was concentrated away from him; so, presumably, would be the attention of the sentries and the rest of the garrison. He brought up his revolver and fired

115

towards the nearest of the perimeter guards. He missed; as the soldier swung his gun round and crouched, the rest of the party opened fire together. This time, the sentry bought it. He crashed to the concrete and rolled over, holding his stomach. The signalman came back from the rise at the double.

'Raised the ship, sir,' he reported breathlessly. 'They answered first time.'

'Thank God for that, anyway,' Cameron said.

Newcombe ran up. 'We'll never do it now, sir! Not enough rifles left to convince a raving loony. Best pull out. There's not a bleeding hope, the whole show's buggered.'

Cameron took a deep breath. Newcombe was probably right. But first there was Kollenborne. Cameron said, 'We have to find the others. They may be heading this way – what's left of them – trying to make contact.'

Newcombe gave a short, bitter laugh. 'Bloody suicide,' he said.

Oleander had lain with engines stopped, drifting in lonely isolation well to seaward off Beni Saf. More sounds of firing had come on the offshore wind. Forrest could hardly keep still. There had been truth in what Perry-Grant had said earlier: to exceed his orders, to act on his own, could ruin everything, yet the temptation was immense. He had guns, he had more men at a pinch, he had a ship beneath his feet. The decision was his alone. The Captain of any ship was a lonely man who could do no more than seek opinions. The sifting of those opinions was the Captain's job. If it was a matter of seamanship, of navigation, there would be no problem; he would know precisely what to do. But currently he was in a dilemma. Go in and maybe wreck the plans, or leave his ship's company to it when he might be able to bring off at least a few of them? Forrest was a seaman and thought as a seaman; that presupposed a concern for life and the saving of it whenever there was even the ghost of a chance. Admirals and politicians didn't see things in quite the same

116

way. They had a war to win or lose and that was all that mattered. Men were expendable and commanding officers at sea had to accept that.

Forrest shifted restlessly. He was aware of Perry-Grant behind him. He could almost smell the man's fear. Perry-Grant knew that Forrest was debating whether or not to take the ship in and to hell with it; and Forrest was aware that he knew. Perry-Grant didn't like gunfire any more than he liked the menace of a gale along an exposed mole. Things travelled aboard a small ship and Forrest had overheard remarks that had indicated panic on Perry-Grant's part as they came under fire on entering Mers-el-Kebir. Remarks, based upon nothing official, could not be acted upon. But as a result Forrest was beginning to feel merciless towards Perry-Grant.

Once again he lifted his binoculars and searched the shoreline, now some four miles to the south and visible only as a blur on low-lying land. As he did so the wireless office called. Forrest took up the phone.

'Captain.'

'Able to receive, sir. We're taking routines, sir.'

'Well done, Parrish! Thank you.' Forrest put down the phone. He gave a sick grin through set teeth. What the hell was the point in being able to receive? No one would be passing orders to them. If only he could transmit and ask for a big drop on the anthrax pits – some of Monty's own Eighth Army and to hell with the ambitions of the Free French command. why should it all be left to the Free French anyway?

'Captain, sir – '

Forrest swung round. 'Yes?'

It was the leading signalman. 'Flash from the shore, sir. Three longs.'

'Right!' Forrest said in a hard voice, sweating with sheer relief. He turned to Perry-Grant. 'Engines to full ahead. Wheel five degrees to port. When the ship has way, steer one-eight-oh. We're going in. And for God's sake pull yourself together.'

The firing from Cameron's party had given away their position, given away the fact that there was another assault group in the vicinity. The German fire had started up in their sector and the searchlight had blazed out towards them. However, they had been just beyond its range and Cameron was able to pull further back to regroup while bullets ripped overhead. Shepherded by Cameron and Newcombe, the party executed a flanking movement north and east towards where they expected to contact any survivors from Kollenborne's group, and keeping beyond the searchlight's probe. Cameron could see Nazi troops mustering, pouring out from some barrack huts and streaming across the concrete pit tops to man the perimeter.

Newcombe said, 'Sods are concentrating on where we just come from. Could leave the northern perimeter clear, with luck. Might make the coast yet, I reckon.'

They crawled on as fast as possible, bodies lacerated on rough stones. The rain was pouring down still, deadening the sound of movement. A few minutes later Cameron passed the word to get up and run. All the Nazi reaction was still concentrated on the south-western sector and the way they were heading seemed clear of opposition. Moving fast now, they came abreast of the watch-tower and its searchlight. That searchlight was still directed towards the sector of the perimeter behind them, and the contrasting darkness was the greater. Cameron was the first to stumble over a body; he went headlong, was pulled to his feet by Newcombe. The leading seaman bent over the body.

He said, 'Dead, sir.'

'Move on, Newcombe.'

There were more bodies. They found no one alive, but the scatter of earth and flesh spoke eloquently of mines. Cameron called a halt. 'No further north,' he said. Looking around, he pointed left. 'We've just about out-flanked. Looks like the village down that way. The village and the port.'

'Try to find a boat, sir?'

'It's about all we can do. And speed's the best defence now. That, and keep as quiet as possible. All set?'

'All set, sir,' Newcombe answered.

'Double out, then. Follow me.'

Newcombe grinned, his face just a smudge in the darkness. 'Know the way to the flippin' port, do you, sir?'

'No.'

'That's honest enough,' Newcombe said, and passed the word to run. Cameron went full belt towards the cluster of small buildings that formed the village, buildings that were becoming faintly silhouetted against the backdrop of the sea beyond. It was a fair bet there wouldn't be any mines so close to human habitation, but every footfall was an agony of apprehension nevertheless. They met no one as they pounded into a smelly street of mean hovels; the Arab population was keeping its collective head down. Then, from a side alley, a steel helmet emerged and a man came out. He was no more than three or four yards ahead, just visible in the darkness. Cameron lifted his revolver, then saw Newcombe racing past. Newcombe took the man with a flying tackle and they both went down. As the rest of the men came up, Newcombe got to his feet. He said, 'Best keep anonymous, sir.'

'Is he dead?'

'As mutton. Broke his neck, stupid sod.' Newcombe was grinning like a devil, sweating into his rain-damp blue serge. 'Drag him clear, sir, right?'

'Where to?'

'Down the alley. Just so he doesn't get seen too soon.' Newcombe bent and grabbed the corpse by the legs and heaved it back into the mouth of the alley, a narrow way between two rows of hovels. As he did so there was the sound of movement in rear of the party, running feet and a rattle of equipment. On Cameron's order the seamen and stokers crowded into the alley and moved fast towards the far end. Half-way along they found another lane running across and Cameron took the party into its cover. The footsteps ran on, past the end of the main alley they had left.

Newcombe sniffed. 'Like living in a bleeding dustcart,' he said. Cameron looked around: the alley seemed to be piled with debris of all kinds, much of it human refuse, and the stench was putrid. In the darkness at the end a dog stood, emitting a low growl; Cameron could imagine the raised hackles as the animal watched the invasion of its dining-room. Meanwhile, they might not have much time; it was urgent that they should get into some sort of cover, temporarily at any rate.

Leading Seaman Newcombe had the same idea and was already moving along the alley's filth, treading warily. In a few moments he came back, fast.

'Posh joint up there, sir,' he reported, jerking his head to the rear. 'Gates and all.'

'Shut?'

'And locked. But we can climb over. No one around. All right, sir?'

Cameron nodded. 'We'll risk it.'

He followed Newcombe along the alley. Posh seemed to be the word: behind the wrought-iron gates was a square with a fountain set among tiles, a very ornate courtyard if seen in daylight. Now there was no light and the place appeared deserted, with no glimmer in the slit windows of the buildings set around.

'Bloody sultan's palace,' Newcombe said. 'Or sheikh, or whatever the local big noise is called. Make a nice messdeck for a bit of kip, that would. Go into the parlour, sir?'

'Fast as you can,' Cameron answered. It took them little time to climb over the gates and drop down into the courtyard and when Cameron was over Newcombe had already found an entry to the building. Going through an archway he had found a gaunt, ancient Arab in a long robe, guarding a door of metal-studded wood. He called to Cameron, who found him with his bayonetted rifle stuck hard against the old man's throat.

120

'Methuselah,' Newcombe said. 'I told him I'd have his guts out if he made a sound. I think he got the drift like. He could have keys on him somewhere below the nightie.'

'Right, I'll search him.'

'Sooner you than me, sir,' Newcombe said cheerfully. 'I reckon he's bloody crawling.'

He was; he was as chatty as a workhouse with lice and with his tongue as well, but none of the seamen could understand a word he said. Cameron had the keys in his hand when a sharp voice came suddenly from the rear, speaking French. They all turned. A tall Arab, seen in the light of a tallow lantern held by another man, stood there with a German pattern automatic rifle aimed towards them. The face was hawkish, dark, with heavy lines driving down from nose to mouth, and a moustache upon the upper lip. In French still, he asked who the intruders were. Cameron gave no answer, hoping even now to play for time. The Arab came closer; so did the man with the lantern. The thin yellow light fell on the seamen's jerseys, on the seaboots with the thick wool of the stocking-tops turned down over the leather.

'Sailors,' the Arab said. He spoke in English now. 'The British Navy, where I expected French soldiers.'

Cameron felt a start of surprise. 'Expected?'

'Yes.' There was a slight smile on the man's face now.

'Then – you know?'

'I know, my friend. I know why you have come to Beni Saf. If you will hand back the keys that you have taken, I shall explain – and I shall refrain from shooting you!' The Arab gave a deep laugh. 'Do not be too surprised at your luck, my friend. The humblest house in Beni Saf would have given you welcome and shelter, for the Nazi plans are now known in the village and well detested. The keys, quickly.' He held out a hand. Cameron returned the keys and the Arab continued, 'I am Sheikh Abdelazziz Brahami, no friend to the Nazis – they believe me to be, but I am not.' He seemed to draw himself straighter. 'I am a former colonel of goums. You have heard of the goums?'

'Yes.' Cameron felt enormous relief. In spite of what the sheikh had said – in spite of the undoubted fact that none of the inhabitants of Beni Saf would want to see their country rendered useless and deadly for generations ahead – there was luck around. The goums were an irregular band of mixed infantry and cavalry, basically bandits, wild men of little discipline and customarily covered with long, dank hair and massive cartridge-filled bandoliers worn over goat-skins, carrying long-barrelled rifles with snaky bayonets, mostly rusty. They were mercenaries but Cameron believed that most of them at any rate had been bought by the Free French rather than by the Nazis.

Abdelazziz Brahami asked, 'Where is Admiral Boulin?'

In the lantern's light Cameron caught Newcombe's eye. Newcombe shrugged. The Arab knew it all. Cameron said, 'Admiral Boulin is dead. So are many men.'

'But many live. That is well. I am glad.'

'You knew Admiral Boulin?

'I am not personally acquainted with him. But it was from me that the first word went to a person in Oran about the anthrax spores. You will trust me?' Abdelazziz Brahami smiled broadly, the eyes glittering. 'A foolish question! You have no option.' He stood to one side and gestured towards a doorway on the far side of the courtyard, still keeping the automatic rifle lined up on the seamen.

12

FORREST was summoned by the sound-powered telephone. He lifted the receiver. 'Captain here.'

'Chief ERA, sir. Got to shut down, sir –'

'Like hell, Chief!'

'Sorry, sir.' The Chief ERA's voice was adamant. 'No option. Matter of minutes before the main steam pipe fractures, sir.'

'Jesus. Isn't there anything you can do?'

'Done it all, sir. No go. Permission to clear the engine-room, sir, please?'

'It's that urgent?'

'Like I said, sir, any minute.'

Forrest said resignedly, 'Go ahead, Chief.'

'Right.' Chief ERA Makins slammed the phone down and nodded at ERA Lott. Lott yelled out: all hands were to get on deck pronto. There was a controlled, disciplined rush for the ladder. Lott found himself feeling surprised that the engine-room should go and get buggered while Gimble was ashore; funny, that. He went up second to last, just ahead of the Chief. The Chief had just got clear when there was a roar of escaping steam from the fracture, which was on the wrong side of the main shut-off valve. The Chief, Lott thought, was dead lucky not to have got a boiled arse. Looking back Lott could see only steam, almost solid, scalding. A few more seconds and they'd all have had it. The skin would have peeled from their bodies.

The Chief went to the bridge, still holding his cottonwaste, badge of his trade. Forrest was in a foul mood. 'Of all bloody times, Chief!'

'Yes, sir. I'm sorry, sir. I know what's at stake.'

Forrest nodded; it wasn't the Chief's fault. 'I realize you did your best. We've done too much steaming, that's the trouble. Overdue for a refit.'

'Yes, sir, that's about it. Not that it should have happened, mind – there's been some lousy work in the yard, sir, back when she was built, I reckon –'

'Well, we won't hold the inquest yet, Chief. How long do I have to hang around?'

'Hard to say yet, sir. Quite a while. I have to let all the steam go to start with. Then I can make a repair, sir.'

'Makeshift job, I suppose?'

'One that'll hold till we can get into Algiers or Gib, sir.'

'All right,' Forrest said. He looked ahead towards Beni Saf. Those poor bloody landing parties, expecting him to move in . . . and dawn was no more than three hours away. If he didn't make it by then, they'd have had it, more than likely. 'Just be as fast as you know how, that's all!'

'I'll be that, sir.' Makins turned away and went down the ladder to the upper deck and thence into the petty officers' mess to pick up some gear and have a quick draw at a fag. The engine-room would take a while to clear itself of steam and cool down. The ship being at action stations, the mess was occupied only by a first-aid party consisting of a solitary supply assistant and the petty officers' messman, a three-badge AB lost in gloomy contemplation of ERA Lott's pin-ups.

'Taking your mind off the war, Stripey?' the Chief ERA asked. He found what he'd come for, lit his fag and drew smoke in deep. The three-badgeman shifted his bottom on the settee and remarked that he was taking his mind off sod all, he was just looking and wondering if women were really like that. The ones he'd known in the home ports hadn't been and though it was different east of Suez he, personally, hadn't been lucky enough. The Chief ERA, who had seen a snapshot of the messman's wife, felt a twinge of sympathy.

124

He finished his cigarette with quick drags, chucked the dog-end in an ashtray, and went back to the engine-room for a look-see.

'You will be safe here,' Sheikh Abdelazziz Brahami said. The British party had been led below ground level, into what had once been a dungeon. It had changed so little from a more gory past that it could be a dungeon still. Chained handcuffs hung from the walls, and stains that looked like rust on the stonework could be age-old blood. There was even a rack thick with dust and cobwebs. Other instruments of torture included thumb-screws, ankle-crushers, and a contraption made of iron lattice-work, such that could be placed over a man's head, and fitted with a wicked barb for insertion in the mouth. In one corner was a dark hole covered with an iron grille. Just below the grille, in the light of the lantern brought in by the sheikh's attendant, a human skull was just visible. There was even a smell of death, musty and vile.

'Suppose there's a search?' Cameron asked.

'You will not be here long. There will be no search while you are here.'

'The Nazis know we're around somewhere,' Cameron pointed out. 'They'll run a toothcomb through the village.'

'Yes,' Abdelazziz Brahami said, smiling, 'but my palace will not be high on the Nazis' list. I am trusted. If they are insistent, which they will not be, I have ways of delaying them for long enough. Do not be anxious. Thanks to the landings, the Nazis are under pressure from other directions also –'

'Have you any news, Abdelazziz Brahami?'

The sheikh smiled again. 'You ask this because you fear the anthrax spores may be used? Yes, I have word. The British and Americans have established their beachheads and are advancing upon Oran. The city is expected to fall to them shortly.' The sheikh paused, eyes flickering. 'I have word that German bombers are coming in soon to land upon the air-strip to the south of the village. There may be little time left.'

'Then – '

'Patience, Lieutenant! I go away now. I shall come back, never fear.'

The Arab withdrew with his attendant, who left the tallow lantern behind on the stone floor. The door, a heavy one, iron-bound, was closed behind them. Cameron heard a lock turned and bolts being shot across.

Gimble asked uneasily, 'Why are they shutting us in, sir?'

'Probably because of the Nazis, Gimble. Don't worry about it.'

'No, sir.' Gimble's lips began to form a circle.

'And don't bloody whistle!' Newcombe said. He caught Cameron's eye and gave a grin. 'Some messdeck, sir. Just like Nelson's wooden walls, all that's missing is the cat.'

'Cat?'

'Cat-o'-nine-tails. And a keel to be hauled round.' Newcombe moved over to the hole in the corner and stood looking down. 'Know what this is, do you, sir?'

Cameron joined him. Looking down he saw that the skull was in fact attached to a complete skeleton, so yellowed with age as to be almost black, and brittle looking. He said, 'No. What is it?'

'*Oubliette*, sir. When I was a nipper, my mum took me on a tour of Warwick Castle. They had an *oubliette*. A hole in the stone, with a grille over it ... anyone who offended His Lordship was shoved down there and just forgotten. Oublietted, see. Frog lingo. Starved to death, all cramped so they couldn't move. Talk about democracy.'

'There wasn't any then.'

'Nor was there more recently for this bloke.' Newcombe pointed down through the grille. 'Makes you think more kindly about chief gunner's mates, I reckon!'

Cameron moved away; the sight of the skeleton, of terrible death, depressed him. They could all be dead soon, and just as horribly if not more so. Suddenly, Newcombe seemed equally depressed, moving restlessly up and down the lantern-lit dungeon. The Navy in peacetime trained you for war and, even if the point wasn't stressed unduly, that included death or anyway its strong possibility if you were unlucky. But not death in this sort of situation, in a wog dungeon or in anthrax-laden air outside. Before the war, the Navy hadn't thought in terms of germs and biological horrors. If you were going to get your lot, it would be in the flash and thunder of the guns, or the sudden explosion of a torpedo or a mine, or down in the depths of the sea's bone-cleansing salt. And of course you didn't think about it anyway, just didn't reckon on it happening. Not when you were boozing-up in Malta, or searching – you didn't need to look very hard – for floozies up the Gut as the Med Fleet called Strada Stretta, or taking part in manoeuvres with the Home Fleet, or an inter-squadron regatta when you pulled your guts out for the honour of the ship and the beer that flowed after the race was won, beer paid for by your Divisional Officer whose efficiency in training you got him in the skipper's good books. And you didn't think about death when you were charging through Hong Kong in a rickshaw pulled by a cringing coolie wearing a funny hat, living for a brief spell like an officer – or like a belted earl with *oubliettes* to take care of people who annoyed you. There had been many times when Newcombe could have done with an *oubliette*, though the chances were his good nature would have got the better of his revenge as he was about to shove the Master-at-Arms down into oblivion ... even Masters-at-Arms probably had a right to live.

Newcombe came back to the present, sharply: there was a distant throb, muffled but unmistakable. That Arab sheikh's information had been spot on. It was the note of the Nazi bombers and it was coming closer, rather sooner than Newcombe had expected when Abdelazziz Brahami had spoken. He felt the sweat start on his body. He said, 'Jesus, where's that bloody Arab?'

'He'll be back.'

'I hope you're right, sir. Time's short. He could be double-crossing us. Or he could have been rumbled by the Nazis.'

'Right,' the Chief ERA said. 'All set, Lotto?'

'All set, Chief. It'll last long enough, I reckon.'

The Chief ERA took a long look around his engine-room and at his depleted staff of stokers. He was proud of the efforts that had been made to repair the fractured pipe; it hadn't taken as long as he'd feared. He went to the starting platform and called the bridge. 'Captain, sir? Chief here. Ready to flash up, sir.'

'Well done, Chief. Get steam soonest possible, report when ready to proceed.'

'Aye, aye, sir.'

On the bridge, Forrest did his best to contain his consuming impatience. He felt a shake in his hands as the wait went on. A matter of minutes after the call from the engine-room he heard the distant, oncoming throb of aircraft.

'Hear that?' he asked.

Perry-Grant said, 'Yes, sir.'

'German.'

'Yes, sir.'

'Approaching from the south, I fancy.'

'Do you intend to open?'

'No, I don't. Not even if they pass within range. I don't want to give away my position so long as I can still take advantage of what's left of the dark.'

'Determined to be the hero of Beni Saf, aren't you?'

Forrest was rocked by the sheer venom of Perry-Grant's tone. Never could he have imagined any officer would reveal his hatred and his own feelings so viciously, so rudely. The man must have lost all control. Forrest couldn't help his reaction. He said evenly, 'I would have thought your instinct to keep safe would have precluded any engagement with enemy aircraft, Grant. You surprise me.'

Perry-Grant said nothing further; Forrest seethed as he listened to the aircraft sounds. There were, he believed, a lot of them, impossible to assess how many from just the sound. It was likely they were heading out to attack the British warships lying off – if they were still lying off at this stage – in support of the operation. That was a nasty thought: it could be – it was – his duty to warn the fleet in case for some reason they hadn't picked them up. With no wireless transmitter working, he could give that warning only by using his ack-ack guns. The bigger consideration should take priority: his own landing party was small. Forrest jutted his chin: family first and bugger it!

Forrest scanned the overcast, glasses elevated, trying to penetrate. No use, couldn't see a thing beyond cloud. The rain beat down soakingly. Then he realized that the aircraft sounds were not getting any closer and that they had thinned out.

He said, 'It's a landing.'

'Then we're lucky,' Perry-Grant said behind him.

'Lucky be buggered. They're going in to load up for the drop, don't you realize that? *The anthrax drop!*' Forrest called the engine-room. 'Chief, it's the eleventh hour. How long'll you be?'

'Doing our best, sir. Not long now.'

'I take it the boilers hadn't cooled right down?'

'Not right down, sir, no.'

The Chief's voice was patient, unhurried. You couldn't hurry engineers because they couldn't hurry bits of metal nor the capabilities of boiler water to absorb heat. No doubt it had been much the same in the days of sail: the wind came when it felt like it and not because you had the enemy in sight. Forrest clenched his fists, the nails dug in deep – drew blood though he didn't know it till afterwards. He was shaking all over now, as though trying to urge the ship from its lethargy by means of his own vital spark. Everything that was in him was concentrated on closing the gap to the shore.

That was when the wireless message came. The leading telegraphist reported to the bridge with a signal in plain language. Addressed to *Oleander*, it read: *You are to withdraw to join support group and come under orders of Captain(D).* The originator was NCXF – Admiral Sir

Andrew Cunningham himself.

Forrest cursed savagely. Perry-Grant gave an opinion, unasked. He sounded happier. He said, 'The fact it's in plain language must mean we have full control of the beaches, of the whole area in fact.'

'Yes. No more danger, Grant. Except in Beni Saf. And that's where we're going.' Forrest screwed the message form into a ball and flung it into a corner of the bridge. He didn't miss Perry-Grant's expression, lit by the dim glow from the binnacle. To reject Cunningham's orders was a serious matter. Perry-Grant didn't argue but his face looked crumpled; he would no doubt ensure that the facts were brought to the attention of authority. Five minutes later the engine-room reported ready.

'Right,' Forrest said forcefully. 'Full ahead, Chief.' He slammed the phone back on its hook. 'Put her on course for Beni Saf, Grant, and warn all guns' crews.'

13

WHEN Abdelazziz Brahami came back he confirmed the landing of the German bomber force. He said, 'You will not have long now. I have spoken to persons that can be trusted, persons who also fear and detest the use of the anthrax spores. It is expected that the bombers will take off with their loads as soon as they have refuelled. The spores will be first disseminated among the soldiers of Montgomery's armies and upon Oran. You must do all that is possible, Lieutenant.'

'We'll do that all right.'

The Arab moved across to the hole in the corner. He said, 'You all follow me.' Bending, he lifted away the grille. Newcombe gave him a hand to drag the skeleton out. The bones dangled, rattling gruesomely.

'Poor sod,' Newcombe said as he dropped them in a heap.

'Thief,' the sheikh said. 'In my father's time.'

'Been there that long?' Newcombe was scandalized.

'With recent interruptions – yes. Since my father's death we have become more enlightened.'

'Just cut off their hands now?' Newcombe asked. Cameron gestured to him to cool it. Newcombe muttered that, talking of cutting things off, he'd heard it was asking for trouble to attempt sexual intercourse in North Africa. Abdelazziz Brahami didn't hear that; he was lowering himself into the hole, not without difficulty. His voice came up, telling the rest of them to follow. The *oubliette* itself ended in solid stone but a narrow gap had been cut in the side wall near the bottom, a gap through which Abdelazziz

Brahami squeezed himself followed by Cameron. The darkness was intense, the light from the tallow lantern, which had been left behind, not penetrating beyond the upper rim of the hole. The sheikh took Cameron's arm.

'Now you are in a tunnel,' he said. 'Soon it will narrow and the height will decrease. You will have to crawl. It will not be easy.'

Cameron asked where the tunnel led.

'To close by the pits of the anthrax spores. The Nazis do not know this. The tunnel was dug out after my father's death, secretly. When first I succeeded him, I had much trouble with rebellious tribesmen ... an escape route was needed should the palace be attacked.' The voice came eerily through the pitch dark. 'The hole in the floor, and the skeleton, kept the secret very well.'

And so, probably, had the project labour force, Cameron thought; they had quite likely been put to death after the job was complete. As the seamen and stokers came through they moved off in single file, keeping their heads low, each of them holding fast to the next ahead. The atmosphere grew stifling, thick and close. Way behind, Cameron heard Leading Seaman Newcombe's voice, oddly flat and muffled: 'Home from home, eh? Just like the double bloody bottoms in a bleeding battlewagon!'

'See anything?'

'No. Not a thing.'

Forrest stared ahead, eyes straining through the rain. The wind was bringing up the spray now; it came back over the bows, flinging into the crew of the 4-inch ack-ack. The visibility was coming down fast – that was lucky enough, for if they were unable to see much from the ship, those ashore could be equally unable to see their approach, although that wasn't to be relied on. There would be a strong degree of watchfulness in Beni Saf – bound to be, after that earlier gunfire.

Forrest couldn't pick up the port or the breakwater,

132

couldn't be sure what if any ships were alongside or riding at anchor inside. It wasn't all favourable: it wouldn't do much good if he piled his ship up and left her helpless under the German guns.

Perry-Grant chose that moment to underline the dangers. 'It's pilotage insanity,' he said. 'If we manage to enter it'll be a miracle, if you ask me.'

Forrest hadn't asked him but held back from the obvious and childish retort. Up to a point the man was right, but he wasn't giving any thought to the hands ashore. Forrest was willing to take any risk now. Even if he grounded, he could still use his guns. And he didn't expect to meet opposition in terms of big-calibre guns. Boulin had said the port was not defended by heavy batteries. The whole defence was based on anonymity, on not attracting British attention. The main opposition would come from men with rifles and automatic weapons.

Something loomed. The starboard lookout called, 'Wall ahead, sir. Breakwater, sir!'

'Full astern – quickly!'

Perry-Grant didn't delay this time. With only a cable's-length to spare the speed, reduced already, came off. Water boiled up below the counter and began to swill for'ard, grey and murky. Forrest ordered port wheel; the ship's head, with sternway on, swung a little to starboard.

'Stop engines.'

The ship was brought up, bows pointing towards the now visible gap in the breakwater, the entry to the port. A few masts could be seen. Small boats only. Perry-Grant asked, 'Well, sir? What do we do now?'

'Stand by to open fire,' Forrest answered. 'I'm holding her off right here until they show what they've got. Then I'll turn us into a moving target.'

'We just haven't the gun power,' Perry-Grant said, his voice shaking. 'There's no point – '

'There's every point. I'm not thinking I can blast the whole bloody port to kingdom come. Haven't you taken it in yet, the idea's a diversion?' Perry-Grant didn't answer; Forrest leaned over the bridge screen. '4-inch, stand by!'

'Stand by, sir.' Forrest recognized the voice of the captain of the gun: Leading Seaman Fitch, steady as a ramrod. Forrest wished Fitch was on the bridge instead of Perry-Grant. Fitch was reliable and would never panic, never run for safety. But Fitch had his number written down ahead. As Forrest passed the order to open fire through the breakwater a stream of tracer arced out and slanted slap into the 4-inch. Fitch was dead before he pitched over the side. After that, everything seemed to open at once. As the 4-inch and the pom-pom started their racket from the corvette, the port came alive with rifles and machine-guns. A lucky hit from the 4-inch took a sandbagged gun position along the break-water, and in the glare of the explosion Forrest watched the fragmentation of bodies as the shrapnel scattered in jags of metal. He put his ship astern with the wheel over to star-board; he passed the orders down himself. Perry-Grant was flat on the deck, his head covered with his arms, a rabbit acting as an ostrich: there was no safety anywhere. Forrest shouted for the searchlight. The beam swept the breakwater and the berths beyond; there was no sign of Cameron's landing party. Forrest had scarcely expected there would be. He could only hope they were in a position to take advantage of what he was doing.

The searchlight went out suddenly, its bulb and reflectors shattered by machine-gun fire. That was that. Before the beam had gone Forrest had seen the military concentration in the little fishing port. Troops were piling from road trans-port that was still coming in from the south, from where Admiral Boulin had said the anthrax storage pits were sited. There was also some unexpected light artillery about to go into action. The crash of it was heard soon after the search-light had died. A shell went overhead, uncomfortably close.

Forrest, at the binnacle, said, 'Stop engines.'

'Stop engines, sir. Engines repeated stopped, sir.'

'Half ahead. Wheel amidships.'

Forrest straightened, looked down at the cowering heap on the deck of the bridge, and called the engine-room. 'Chief. Captain here. How's that pipe?'

'Holding, sir. She'll be all right.'

'Thank God something is. I'm standing out a little, Chief. I'll keep up the gunfire so as to hold the Nazis down by the harbour. I'll be altering course and speed fairly often. Everything else all right below?'

'Everything's fine, sir. Short-handed, that's all.'

Forrest put the phone back. As they moved outwards the effect of the gunfire began to lessen and Forrest believed the Germans had lost their target. He said, 'On your feet, Grant. It's safe now. For a while, anyway.

Perry-Grant sat up. His steel helmet had rolled away; he reached for it and put it on. He looked abject. Forrest felt contempt but also pity. If a man hadn't guts, there wasn't much he could do about it, it was a fact of nature. But fear was not best coped with by softness and there was ice in Forrest's voice as he said, 'Stand up, Grant. Take a grip. There's work to be done. For a start, I want a count of casualties and a report of any damage. I want it at once, before I go in again. Understood?'

Slowly, Perry Grant got to his feet and stood unsteadily, holding on to the binnacle. He said, 'Yes.'

'Then get on with it.'

They had crawled a long way through the tunnel and the air had grown staler by the minute. At the tail of the line Stoker Second Class Gimble believed his last hour was about to come. During his all-too-short training ashore, Gimble had spent a forenoon aboard a battleship that had come alongside in Devonport dockyard for repairs. The Commander(E) in charge of training had decided it would be a good idea to take advantage of the presence of a battleship to let his trainees see what a capital ship's engine-rooms – there were four of them – felt like. Gimble had been impressed and scared: it was all so huge, so filled with networks of steel ladders, with bank upon bank of dials and gauges, with hundreds of polished brass hand-wheels stuck on stalks, some long, some short. From each engine-room a great long tunnel had led aft and through it had driven an immense, shiny, steel shaft, the main shaft that connected the engine to the screw and turned it at an unbelievable speed. That tunnel had looked like the road to hell, something to be feared. The chief stoker had made some of the trainees crawl along it and had brought up the rear himself, right behind Gimble, a solid chief petty officer blocking all escape. Like that skeleton in the hole.

Gimble shuddered.

You couldn't really compare this place with the battleship's main shaft tunnel – for one thing the latter had been electrically lit and there was the shaft running through it, fortunately not turning whilst in harbour – but the claustrophobic feeling was the same, not to say much worse. The darkness alone ... and the not knowing where they were going, except that it was in the direction of the filth in the pits. Some of those spores could have escaped; the tunnel might be full of them. There was plenty of dust that filled Gimble's throat and lungs every time he breathed. He believed after a while that he was going to suffocate. He had felt that aboard the battleship. While he and his mates had been in the long steel tunnel there had been an air raid on Plymouth. Gimble had heard the crump of bombs and felt them too; the battleship had shuddered to the fall of a close one in the dockyard. He'd had a job not to scream, to show his near panic. He'd whistled instead, until told to can it. When the order had come to clear the tunnel, he had pressed back but had been brought up short by the bulk of the chief stoker. Something altogether ludicrous had happened. The chief stoker was a very fat man, too fat to turn round, so he'd had to back out. In so doing he had become attached to one of the bridge-like steel clamps that stopped the shaft, when spinning, from jumping out of its seating. His jacket had rucked up and his braces had become hooked on some projection and there had been a long delay while the bombs continued to fall and the chief stoker struggled free of his braces. Gimble had almost sweated blood.

As, now, he moved in rear of the others along this much worse tunnel, he heard the sound of gunfire from somewhere in the rear. It was muffled but it had the feel of a very big barrage. Gimble's feeling of suffocation increased as he went on. Very soon after the start of the gunfire, the tunnel began to shake and, again muffled, he heard motor sounds, heavy vehicles on the move.

It was like Devonport again. Gimble stopped. He had to get out. He moved back along the way he had come. He didn't want to be trapped; and he knew the way out. Whimpering with the onset of panic, he retreated fast. At the head of the line, Cameron made an accurate guess as to what was happening up in the open air. He communicated this to Abdelazziz Brahami.

'The ship that brought you, Lieutenant?' the Arab asked.

'Yes. How far to go now?'

'There is little more.'

They moved on; just two minutes later the Arab halted. He said, 'Now we are in a wider space and nearly at the end of my tunnel. Bring up all your sailors, quickly. I shall explain what you will find outside.'

Cameron passed the word along to muster. They came together in a bunch. Newcombe, who had made a count, reported to Cameron. 'One missing, sir. Gimble.'

'Oh, bloody hell – '

'I'll go back and look, sir.' Newcombe moved away but Cameron called him back. No time, he said. They couldn't hold things up now. Without delay Abdelazziz Brahami gave them the lie of the land to which they would emerge. The tunnel's end, he said, was effectively disguised. It emerged not immediately into the open air but into a large recess in a hillside, a place currently in use by the Germans as a store. The actual entry from the tunnel to the recess was through what appeared to be a blank wall of sandstone.

'You will see,' he said. 'The wall will move aside. There will be no difficulty. When you leave the store, you will find the pits some half a mile to the right. To the left are barrack huts used by the German soldiers. Because of your Captain's action, they are likely to be empty now. There are no heavy gun emplacements around the base. I believe you will have little difficulty in establishing control.'

'And after that?'

'Perhaps that can be left to your Captain.'

'To call for a support force? He can't. The ship's out of wireless communication.'

Abedelazziz Brahami said, 'No matter. If he had not come, other methods would have been needed and these will be used. As soon as you leave the cave, I shall return along the way we came and I shall send a messenger to Fort Mersel-Kebir, where I have good friends. Do not worry, Lieutenant.'

'But if your messenger's taken by the Germans?'

'He will not be. He knows the country. The Germans think they know it, but they do not.'

Gimble ran like the wind. He hadn't been seen as he left the sheikh's palace and he ran for the only safety he knew: the shore. If he could make the shore a little east of the harbour, he would get in and swim. The *Oleander* was somewhere out there, he knew that, and it might have been the *Oleander* that was responsible for the awful racket of the guns. That was still going on. If he had to die, Gimble would rather it was far, far away from the anthrax. It was worth the chance. In order to move faster Gimble shed his encumbrances: his rifle and webbing equipment. He chucked them down in the alley. There was no one about; the natives were still keeping their heads down, anonymous behind their shut doors.

At the end of the alley Gimble ran slap into a German patrol. Literally. Just as he reached the corner, a soldier came round and they met. They both went down and Gimble was hauled to his feet by the NCO in charge and a gun muzzle was rammed into his stomach.

In English the NCO said, 'Britisher. British pig.' With his free hand he pulled at Gimble's jersey. 'Sailor. The others. Where?' He dug in harder with the gun. 'Tell or I kill.'

Gimble was almost in tears. He shook with fear. He said 'You can't do that.'

'Why?'

'Geneva Convention.' Gimble had heard about that somewhere; it was his protection. Governments, even Hitler's, respected it. 'I'm a POW, aren't I?'

There was a laugh. 'You surrender?'

'Yes. Yes, I surrender. There! Now you've got to treat me proper. I won't give no trouble. Promise.'

The NCO laughed again and flung Gimble against the wall behind, so hard that every bone in his body protested. 'Stupid boy. Now you will come with me. There will be questions, and you will answer them.'

Gimble was surrounded and marched out towards the main alley, the one by which he had entered Beni Saf with Mr Cameron, he believed. In the light of the gun flashes he was able to see that it led down towards the harbour. All hell was being let loose there. There were big flashes coming from seaward, followed by explosions on the shore, and as the patrol moved along a searchlight came on out at sea. It shone right on to the marching patrol, blindingly, straight down between the hovels of the port. It blinded Gimble all right and probably blinded the Nazis at the same time. One of them lurched into the wall and another tripped and fell; and Gimble took his chance, surrender or not. He ran once again. Bullets zipped past him but then the searchlight went out and the resultant dark was intense enough to throw off the pursuit. Gimble dodged round a corner and continued running. He didn't know where, but soon the mean dwellings petered out and he saw that he was coming down to the shore, with the harbour breakwater on his left. He ran on to the water's edge. It was bloody dark. He couldn't see any ship. He was breathing like a steam engine, partly from his exertions, partly from his fear. If he was recaptured now, they would really have a go at him. The Geneva Convention had something to say about prisoners-of-war who broke away and it wasn't encouraging. Aloud, he cursed the darkness. He felt certain the *Oleander* was out there and he didn't doubt the skipper would come in to pick him up if only he could be seen.

Then he found something. Something looming close through the dark, just a blur really, in the lee of the break-water. It was moving slowly up and down and there was a gurgle of water. A man was lying over it, Gimble believed. He was very still. It took Gimble some minutes to realize the man was as dead as mutton and the object was a boat of some sort.

Carefully, his heart in his mouth but his overwhelming desire to get to hell off the beach overcoming fear, Gimble moved closer. The man was dead all right, so was his mate, who was dangling into the water with his head under. Both corpses were in German Army uniforms and the craft was an amphibious one. Gimble had reservations about his ability to steer, but his training had equipped him, rudimentarily, to deal with engines.

No time to lose.

Gimble climbed in, shoved the corpses clear, and started up. No trouble; the soldiers must have been about to move off when they'd been hit from the *Oleander*.

Cameron was doubtful as to whether Abdelazziz Brahami's messenger could make it through the German lines but he was committed now and there was nothing to be done about it. He was in the outer cave now, the German store; the sliding wall had slid, though not so easily as the Arab had forecast. It was a long time since it had been motivated and things had jammed up a little and it had operated in a cloud of dust and sand and not without some horrible creaking, but this had remained unheard.

As he came cautiously into the open Cameron saw that he

needn't have worried about noise: the base was deserted except for the perimeter guards, who were at a safe distance. Cameron's party was now well within the perimeter and keeping close to the walls of the base buildings. Distantly there was light and in it Cameron could see the Nazi bombers on the air-strip, awaiting their loads of canisters. For the present, the loading operation had been suspended. Inside the base, lorries and trucks were waiting, all of them unmanned. Four petrol carriers also waited, no doubt to take fuel to the bombers. It was an extraordinary scene of deserted readiness with all the troops moved out to the vicinity of the harbour; and it might not last, though the battle was in fact still going on.

'Dead easy,' Newcombe said, 'though what we'd have faced if the fun hadn't started up, I wouldn't bloody care to say.'

'Me, too. That sheikh must imagine the British are supermen!'

'Not far wrong, sir.'

Cameron grinned. 'Don't get over-confident.' He was still making a recce. At the nearer of the pits he could see an obvious entrance with steps leading down from ground level, surrounded with a blast wall and sandbags. The entry stood wide open, with light coming through, all ready for loading the bombers. Nasty: if just one of the canisters should come to grief, the effect could be appalling. Cameron said, 'We'll have to be bloody careful with the rifles.' He indicated the entry.

'I take your meaning, sir. Don't worry, I don't want to die, nor does anyone else. Supermen aren't necessarily heroes. What's the next move, sir?'

Cameron said, 'Start a diversion.'

'*Another* one?'

'Wrong choice of word, Newcombe. Start something to bring the sentries in.'

'So we can pick 'em off?'

'Yes.'

Newcombe lifted a hand towards their right. 'Gate guard down there, not paying enough bloody attention to their job. All eyes on the port. Start with them, sir?'

'It's as good as anything else,' Cameron said. 'How's your target practice?'

'It'll do,' Newcombe answered briefly. 'There's a light in the guardroom window, see it, sir? Sooner or later some daft sod's going to move across it.' He paused. 'I reckon I'd do better to nip in closer. Get over by that barrack hut. All right, sir?'

Cameron nodded. Newcombe moved fast, flitting like a ghost across the cluttered space between. Cameron lost sight of him once he had sunk into the lee of the hut. Soon after he had gone, a man's head was silhouetted against the light. In the same instant Newcombe fired. The glass shattered; so did the head. Blood obscured the jagged splinters. The light remained on. Within a minute a bulge formed against the guardroom's door jamb and Newcombe fired again. The body fell outwards. Newcombe was seen running back. As he rejoined Cameron he said breathlessly, 'Sentries on the move, sir. If we nip round the back we can pick some of 'em off as they come in. If we can get the lot, we may have time to sabotage the flippin' bombers an' all.'

Cameron didn't comment. Time wasn't on their side. There was an increasing feeling that they'd taken on the impossible. They might kill the sentries and establish a kind of control but it couldn't last once the base command ticked over and the troops were brought back from the harbour diversion. All he could hope for was that the warships lying further out at sea would have cottoned on by now that fighting was going on in Beni Saf and would report to the Commander-in-Chief. His own part in this was just to hold on and prevent the loading of the bombers – if he could. Probably he wouldn't get the chance. There was a lot he wanted to say to Newcombe and the others before the end came, but he was unable to find the words.

142

14

ABOARD the headquarters ship of the Centre Task Force, *HMS Largs*, the absence of *Oleander* from the support group had been noted. It was not certain that the corvette had received the signalled orders from NCXF; there had been no acknowledgement, and the fact remained that she had not acted in obedience to the signal. There could be just two reasons for that: W/T unserviceable or the corvette had been sunk by enemy action whilst engaged on her special mission for the Free French command. If the latter should be the case, there might be survivors. A destroyer, *HMS Pindari*, was despatched with orders to investigate the sea area between Cape Fegalo and a point to the west of Beni Saf. As *Pindari* passed westwards of Cape Fegalo, she picked up evidence of fighting well ahead off Beni Saf. A little later, while still east of the port, a small craft was sighted, wallowing in heavy seas. Gimble had been blown well off his track by a strengthening wind. Expecting survivors, *Pindari* altered course.

Gimble was brought aboard, grinning with relief when he saw British ratings but green with sea-sickness. It had been a rough ride. He was wrapped in blankets and then taken to the bridge to report in person to the Captain, a Commander RN.

'Who are you?' the Captain asked.

'Name of Gimble, sir, Stoker Two. *HMS Oleander*, sir, corvette, sir – '

'Yes. Just you?'

'Well . . . yes, sir. I left the others ashore, like. I know I didn't ought to, sir, but – '

'Just a moment, Gimble.' The Captain, Gimble thought, sounded toffee-nosed. 'Was your ship sunk?'

'Oh no, sir! That is, I don't think so, sir.'

'You don't *think* so?'

'No, sir. I hadn't been aboard for some while, sir.'

'I think,' the Captain said forebearingly, 'you'd better start at the beginning, hadn't you?'

Cameron's party had moved round the back of the building that was giving them cover. Two of the German sentries had been picked off by the rifles. That had halted the advance, at any rate temporarily. Newcombe said, 'The others'll stay in their sectors, sir, I reckon, in case we've got mates waiting for 'em to move. They won't know how many there are of us. How bloody *few*, that is.'

'Yes. If we can keep them sort of pinned down for long enough – '

'We'll make it, sir.'

Cameron was grateful for the confidence in Newcombe's voice but his doubts were increasing fast. There was no way round the fact that numerically his party was a pathetic little force, or would be if the Nazis should pull back from the port. This they might do at literally any moment, and only a miracle could bring in the Allied armies in time. The prospect of that wasn't worth even a passing thought. In the meantime the anthrax remained in the pits. Whatever might or might not happen to themselves, those spore-canisters would remain until they were loaded aboard the waiting bombers.

Cameron looked across at the apparently unassailable expanse of concrete, at the rows of bug-like ventilator cowls that crawled across. There was a slight lightening of the sky now, just enough to show the glistening wet roofs as the rain continued, blown by the wind's buffet and bluster. He looked at the open doors. Presumably the Nazis had been confident enough that no one would want to venture into an athrax store-house . . .

Something was forming in his mind. Something that would have to be done very quickly.

'Ship on the port quarter, sir, approaching. Destroyer, I think, sir.'

'Right.' Forrest swung his glasses. It was pretty dark yet but he was able to recognize her outline. 'One of ours. We can do with some help.' He saw the flash from a blue-shaded Aldis. The signalman read it off and reported. '*Pindari*, sir.' In return, Forrest made his own number.

The destroyer, approaching at speed, put her engines astern as she came up, drawing level along *Oleander*'s port beam, very dashing in the breaking water. Forrest said sardonically, 'The cavalry of the seas they call them. He's probably come to chase me up for not obeying orders.'

A moment later the destroyer's loud hailer came on and a voice said, 'I have one of your ratings aboard. Stoker Gimble.'

'Good God,' Forrest said involuntarily. He called back, 'How come?'

The destroyer Captain passed a brief summary of a very long story about a tunnel: Gimble liked an audience. The Captain added, 'I've made a signal to NCXF. Air drop of troops most urgent.'

'Many thanks,' Forrest called back, much relieved. 'My W/T has had it.'

'That explains why you haven't withdrawn, I suppose. Cunningham – '

'I know. I'm able to receive but not transmit. I didn't withdraw because I had other things to see to.'

A chuckle came across. 'You can tell that to NCXF himself.'

And balls to NCXF, Forrest said beneath his breath. Aloud he called back, 'Are you going to help out here – help the bombardment?'

'What do you think?' There was a pause. 'Better stuff your

fingers in your ears, old chap! I have *guns*.'

Forrest didn't mind the rudery: he was well aware of the limitations of his own pop-gun armament. Because he intended to enter the port and didn't expect to be able to bring the *Oleander* out again, he asked *Pindari*'s captain to take off his wounded men before opening fire.

'Make it bloody fast,' came the reply. Forrest wasted no time; a boat was called away and, with the French doctor, the casualties were transferred in a couple of short trips, the destroyer coming as close alongside as she could. The moment they were all aboard *Pindari* swung away under full helm, heeling sharply as the thrust of her engines came on. She moved clear and then opened with a broadside. Forrest saw a shell take the breakwater, which erupted in orange flame and a great shower of smashed stone. More shells were flung into the harbour; it became like day. Fires started, red and angry, and vehicles were seen to be ablaze. It was, Forrest began to feel, a mixed blessing. Under too much bombardment the Germans might pull back towards the anthrax base and Cameron's party would be caught out as they emerged from Gimble's tunnel. He called the signalman.

'Make to *Pindari*, suggest holding off now. Intend making an approach on my own to keep them tied down but not too anxious about their base.'

The signal was flashed across. The reply said *Pindari* would be ready to cover. Forrest was grateful for instant understanding. He looked at Perry-Grant. 'I'm taking her right in. Keep your eyes skinned for obstructions.' There was no response; Perry-Grant stood there like a mummified corpse. Forrest took the ship himself. Down the voice-pipe he said, 'Starboard ten, engines full ahead.' Then he called the engine-room and told the Chief ERA his intentions. He added, 'Gimble's back, or almost. I haven't got the story in detail yet, but in my opinion he's due for a medal.'

Makins was stunned. He said, 'Well, chase me round a mulberry bush.'

Cameron asked, 'Can you drive, Newcombe?'

'Car, sir? Yes.'

'Good. Not a car.' Cameron pointed towards the pits. 'Those petrol tankers – see?'

Newcombe swung round. 'Yes. But – '

'I'll take one, you take another. I'll drive mine to the nearer pit, the nearest of the entrances. You take yours to the other pit. There are hoses on the tankers ... soon as they're alongside the open doors, we connect the hoses with the ends led into the pits, and start pumping. Then we fire into the petrol. Got it?'

'Well, I've got it, sir, but in a manner of speaking I haven't.' Newcombe pushed back his steel helmet and wiped at his forehead. 'Will the canisters burn, and will fire kill the spores?'

'I don't know! But the canisters must be made to split open on impact when they're dropped, so they'll be reasonably fragile and may be susceptible to heat. As to killing the spores, well, fire kills most things. It's the best we can do.'

'There'll be a bloody explosion inside. It'll lift the concrete.'

Cameron gave a tight grin. 'Shouldn't do that. The concrete's built to take bombs outside so it won't be too worried about what happens inside.'

'We hope!'

'That's right. Come on. Let's get those tankers into position.'

'Very good, sir. And the hands?'

'All the rest stand by to deal with the perimeter sentries and anyone else who shows up from the harbour.' Cameron paused. Newcombe had drawn a sharp breath and was looking towards the main gate into the base. 'What's up?'

'Listen,' Newcombe said.

Cameron listened. He heard a distant rumble, the sound of transport on the move, coming closer. 'Fast as you can,' he said, and went out at the rush with Newcombe behind him.

He reached one of the pit entrances and flung himself down the steps between the sandbagged blast walls for a quick recce. The place was stacked with the canisters in cardboard cartons: he could see the extent of it in the glow from widely spaced police lights around the walls. A whole lot of death, and it left an unclean feeling. With the door open behind him, Cameron ran full belt for the petrol as Newcombe, in the cab of one of the tankers, drove up and at once jumped down and ran to unstow the big hose. As he did so firing came from the perimeter: someone, possibly the bomber crews, had guessed what was happening when they saw the tanker move towards the pits. With no time to delay, Cameron climbed aboard the second tanker and drove it fast into position. Like Newcombe he unstowed the hose and ran with its end to the open entry. He was scarcely aware of the renewed gunfire from the port or of the now close rumble of heavy German Army vehicles closing in towards the main gate. He dragged the hose as far into the pit as its length would allow and set the end securely in place, the nozzle nipped between two metal racks, the racks that held the cardboard cartons. Leaving the door closed far enough not to nip the hose, he ran back to the tanker. As he did so, there was a shout from Newcombe.

'All ready, sir!'

'Right. Start pumping.'

Newcombe waved again in acknowledgement. Within half a minute Cameron had his own hose in action. It heaved like a lazy snake, straightening the kinks in the heavy-duty canvas. Running back down the steps, he checked inside: all looked well. The petrol, aviation spirit with a low flash point, was gushing out nicely, a strong stream saturating the cartons and filling the air with its fumes. He could only guess at how long the tanker would take to empty. He was going back up the steps when the first of the returning vehicles came through the gateway with its load of Nazi troops. Remaining in the cover of the blast wall, he brought his revolver from its holster.

Oleander was close now to the eastern arm of the break-water. Forrest was handling his ship in the light of the many fires, intending, if possible, to put her alongside and blaze away with every gun that would fire. If necessary, with *Pindari* giving her cover, he would try to land and fight through towards Cameron. He still had some twenty hands available and if the corvette had to be left to be blown up by the Germans, so be it. Men were more important than one corvette that had already done too much sea-time and was prematurely aged.

Now they were nearly in and heading into concentrated fire from the shore. Forrest noted with satisfaction that he was pinning down a pretty large number of soldiers. Watching his course closely, he said, 'Stop engines.' The way began to come off. On the fo'c'sle the 4-inch was flinging shrapnel through the harbour mouth. As the corvette came past the shattered eastern arm, a body of troops opened with automatic rifles and were answered by the pom-pom and the 20mm close-range weapons. Nazi uniforms pitched over into the water. Not enough of them: along the port side of the ship, gunners died as the German fire ripped across. Bullets came over the bridge as Forrest gave his helm orders to avoid the wrecks. He felt sudden pain in his left arm, felt the slow drool of blood. They moved on, the engines now at slow speed, as Forrest felt his way past shattered boats. The din was appalling, the air was filled with tracer, with the racket from a 105mm howitzer that had been set up behind its limber on the inner quay. Its flashes lit the small Arab dwell-ings fronting the water, the hovels of once peaceful fishermen. Forrest was visited by a strange thought: what would Jane think if she could see him now, standing on his bridge like some latter-day Boy on a Burning Deck, going obstinately to his death? For he believed that was going to happen; and his ship, his command, was burning now. A hit from the 105mm had smacked into the fo'c'sle mess deck via the bows. His anchors had gone, the fo'c'sle was lifted so far

149

back that it had now curled almost right over the 4-inch, which could no longer bear ahead, and the messdeck was blazing up through the shattered deck plating. He must look like a roman candle on the move. He hadn't been aware of the steel splinters that had been flung across the bridge, wasn't aware that Perry-Grant had found no safe shelter in the lee of the bridge screen, had got instead a stomach-full of jagged steel that had gutted him like a kipper and left him with his mouth open and his eyes staring, sightless, through the glaze.

Through it all, Forrest put his ship, or what was left of it, neatly alongside the quay. He spoke to the wheelhouse. 'What's it like down there?'

Petty Officer Bowling answered. 'Fair mess, sir.' He sounded badly shaken. 'Fire's breaking through.'

'Get out, Bowling, leave it.' Forrest called the engine-room. 'All up, Chief.'

'You abandoning, sir?'

Forrest grinned savagely from a smoke-blackened face. As he lifted a hand to clear sweat from his eyes he found that his uniform hung in tatters. He said, 'I'm forming a landing party, Chief. All hands.'

'Very good, sir.'

'One last order, Chief: finished with engines.'

Below, the Chief ERA left the starting platform, giving the order to get everyone up. He thought, poor old bugger, he didn't like saying that. They all knew it was for the last time. As they came up on deck, oil-streaked and mostly dead scared, the heavier guns of the *Pindari* opened from seaward, flinging shells on to the village behind the port. One landed close, almost singeing Lott's hair from his head, and he gave a yell as stones flew, clanging on the ship's metal. It had done some good, though: that Jerry 105mm had gone and there was just a hole left where it had stood, and the hole was draped with stripped flesh and limbs that had come adrift. And the rest of the Jerries were starting to bugger off.

150

It was a good moment to put the landing party ashore; Forrest took full advantage of it. Before leaving, he made a final signal to *Pindari*: he was going to fight through to the base and didn't want to be blown up by British guns. Even as that signal was being flashed the scream of shells was heard passing overhead. Forrest thought: if those projectiles hit the pits, we've all had it.

There had been shouting from the perimeter sentries and Cameron, peering over the blast wall, saw the German bomber crews racing down towards the pits. The incoming soldiers were hesitating by the guardroom; they hadn't quite ticked over so far, and an NCO was inside, probably using the telephone after finding the bodies of the gate-guard detail. The stench of petrol was strong now, must surely be wafting over towards the Germans. There was a good deal of uncertainty around by the look of it. Once again the racket from the harbour had increased, was worse now than it had been before. *Oleander* must have been reinforced.

As he watched from his cover, as the petrol continued its flow down into the pit behind him, the troops started to fan out and advance slowly behind their automatic weapons. It looked like the end; Cameron drew back the cocking lever of his service revolver. Whether or not the tanker was still more than half full, he might not have another chance. But something supervened: something exploded smack in the middle of the advancing Nazis and when the smoke cleared away they were all on the ground, some of them screaming. Seconds later another shell exploded in Cameron's rear, beyond the pit where Newcombe was pumping down his load of aviation spirit. The bomber crews appeared to run slap into it. After that the heavy firing stopped. The Nazis seemed completely stunned by now. Cameron moved up the steps and called to Newcombe.

'Here, sir.'

'How's it going?'

'Not far off empty I reckon, sir.'

'We'll make a real bonfire of it. Get all hands back to the pits to form a screen. Then we'll put the other two tanker loads in, all right?'

'All right, sir.' Newcombe sent a shout ringing out to the naval ratings and ran from the further pit, making towards another of the tankers. Cameron did likewise as the British party re-mustered between the pits and the main gate, going down on their stomachs behind their rifles. A few shots came across from the base defenders, smacking into the concrete behind. As Cameron flung himself into the cab of the tanker, a bullet grazed his shoulder and threw him heavily to the floor. He pulled himself up, got the vehicle in motion and swung it, moving fast, for the pit entrance. Jumping down, he fixed the fresh hoses. As he secured the end inside the pit and ran back to set the pump in motion, there was another diversion down by the gate. More firing, and the handful of Nazis left alive were running fast, away from the gate, past the pits for what safety they could find.

Two minutes later a ragged body of men in British naval uniform was seen moving in. Newcombe gave them a cheer, and Cameron saw Forrest stumble and fall as a rifle cracked from the retreating Germans. One of the seamen ran forward as Forrest lurched upright. He didn't appear badly hurt. Cameron didn't wait for the second tanker to empty into the pit. He ran out and disconnected the hose then, once again, he called to Newcombe.

'We'll call it a day. Fire into the juice when you've stopped the pump.'

'Aye, aye, sir.'

They both opened fire at almost the same moment. Cameron was sent flying backwards by the force of the reaction as the aviation spirit went up. There was no chance to shut the door. As he pulled himself back up the steps, his clothing alight, Cameron saw the flame shoot into the sky, saw the thick black smoke curling from the bug-like vents on top of the pits. There was a deep roaring sound and everything appeared to glow red, a devil's glimpse of hell.

Nothing, surely, could live through that.

They were taken off by *Pindari* after troops from Algiers had been dropped and had surrounded what was left of the base, keeping a prudent distance from any possible contamination until the medics and scientists came in to give clearance. The seamen and stokers, three of them supporting Forrest, straggled down to the port, too weary to march; *Oleander* was burning herself out as *Pindari* entered, moving warily through the harbour's wreckage. There were lumps in many throats as they sailed away, both for those who had died and for the old corvette herself. Forrest, it turned out later, was worse than had been thought: a bullet had embedded in his lungs and he was coughing blood; but *Pindari*'s doctor believed he had a fair chance. He was transferred as quickly as possible to a hospital ship, whence he would go to the base hospital in Gibraltar. Cameron and the other survivors, Gimble included, were put aboard the depot ship that had now entered Mers-el-Kebir; and a week later Cameron was in charge of a number of trucks that took *Oleander*'s survivors into Oran for a very special ceremony. In the city's main square, outside the *hôtel de ville*, the tricolour of Free France was to be raised once again in place of the discredited emblem of the Vichy government.

It was a very French occasion.

On parade that emotional day were detachments of zuoaves and spahis of the Corps d'Afrique together with the grotesque-looking goums, killers to a man, crawling with lice and smelling evilly. Alongside Cameron stood Stoker Second Class Gimble with Leading Seaman Newcombe, the Chief ERA and ERA Lott with forty-two seamen and stokers all told; all that were left now. The square was packed to capacity with French civilians, men and women whose home was French North Africa. Gimble was impressed; never had he taken part in the making of history. It would be something to shoot a line about in Pompey, when he got back there. The tricolour crept up the flagstaff. Those in uniform saluted as a military band struck up the *Marseillaise*. There was scarcely a dry eye amongst that crowd. Gimble began to whistle in tune to the *Marseillaise*. Newcombe rounded on him, none too quietly.

'Put a sock in it, you daft little ha'porth, all this bullshit *means* something to the Frogs.'

Cameron's embarrassment was acute, but fortunately no one was taking any notice.